Throne of Obsession

emily bowie

Contents

Chapter 1: Sienna

♥

Not a single person moves for me as I push my way through the overcrowded clubhouse. I'm forced to zigzag around the bodies cramped into the small area. *Is all of America in this tiny room?*

It smells of cigarettes, marijuana, and exhaust—like someone left their bike idling inside. My stomach turns at the smell and I try to breathe as little of it in as possible.

The men look down at me like I'm a nobody. It's how my father has trained them since I was about twelve years old, but I don't miss a few side-eyed looks after I pass. I try to keep my head straight as I step over a girl who is on her knees sucking off the vice president of my father's motorcycle club. The men holler and make fun of me for not staying for the show.

My eyes accidentally slide to the girl and the men cheer. She's my age, and he's...well...he's my father's best friend, has been since they were four.

I try to stay far away from events like these, knowing nothing good ever comes from them. With my father being who he is, I'm not afraid of these men. I'm untouchable to them, but that doesn't mean they wouldn't take if I gave them an inch.

Without knocking, I walk into my father's office. I blow out a breath when I see it's just him. You never know, sometimes. "You texted saying you wanted to see me." I stand tall, trying to look calm when I'm anything but. Despite my best efforts, my hands pick at the edges of my thumbnail, pulling at any loose skin around the nail.

My father looks at my hands and back at me, his disapproval painfully apparent. Immediately, I stop my fidgeting and look him in the eye. Being summoned here is not good. I control my breathing in through the nose and out through the mouth, consciously trying not to make a sound.

For a moment, my father's forehead ruffles into a frown before it's ironed out, looking perfectly flat. "Yes. You're going to want to sit for this." He motions to the chair in front of his desk. I look at it, then back at my father's serious face. His eyes used to hold warmth, but over the years they have grown lifeless. The death of my mother was the first time I saw a flicker of emptiness in them.

"I'm good standing." My heart thunders as his eyes dim further, driving his soul from his body. No matter how hard I focus on my breathing, my muscles clench, and my shoulders turn into rocks as I wait.

He nods and walks around his desk. "You will marry Jack Pierce this summer."

My jaw drops as I hear the vice president's name. "The old guy who's dick is being sucked by a girl younger than me. That guy?" Obviously, I know who Jack Pierce is, and there's no way in Hell I'm touching that guy.

My father's hand flinches as he holds himself back from hitting me. The sound of my swallow is louder than it should be as my entire body cramps tightly from anxiety. If I were anyone else, my cheek would be red.

My father clears his throat, lowering his hand. "There's been tension in the club and this will help bring us all together again."

Ah, yes, the club. It always comes first. I'm stunned into silence. I never expected my father to use me to his advantage. He leans back on his desk, grabbing his red solo cup, and finishes the beer in it with one gulp.

We stand in a stare off until I can find my tongue once again. "He has a son my age. Why not him?" I cross my arms, trying to appear strong.

My father blows out a breath, and suddenly, he looks old and tired. I'm used to seeing the tyrant of the motorcycle club; he hasn't been in father mode for years now. "I already signed the contract. This is your engagement party." I swear I can detect regret and sorrow, but it could be me imagining what I'd like his reaction to be. Growing up, I used to fantasize about being part of a normal, loving family who shared dinner together. Instead, it was me and a stuffed animal, sitting around a spray-painted circle.

"The deal is finalized and going back on it would be civil war." His voice is back to being hard and leaves no room for negotiations.

My mouth opens and my head springs backwards. Unbelievable. There's no use arguing, because once there are signatures, there's nothing I can do about it. I turn on my heels and walk straight out. The moment I walk out of the room, I'm lifted up and the smell of whisky and perfume assaults my senses.

"Cheers to my new fiancée!" Jack hollers, and the room explodes with celebration.

"I'd rather kill you, than marry you!" I seethe in a low, hushed voice only he can hear, pushing myself out of his grasp. His hand holds my shoulder, his fingers digging in painfully. I refuse to cower and give him that power over me.

His lips are at my ear when he says, "Sounds like we're already a married couple."

I rip out of his grip and storm through the house, hearing him yell, "Hear that, boys? She wants to kill me." They laugh at my back, at me.

I can't get out of here fast enough. It doesn't matter who it is, I push people out of my way, step on feet, and forcefully shoulder my way through. My head is down as I maneuver to get back outside into the fresh air. The breeze from outside claws at my hot skin, and I know I'm almost there.

I barrel right into a person, but unlike everyone else, they don't budge. "Move, asshole," I grumble, stomping down on their foot to clear space for myself.

The idiot stays frozen and I have to move around them. Breaking out into the yard, I'm able to take a deep breath. My clothes will probably smell like the house and I'm going to have to wash them and my hair to smell half decent.

Max Mancini

M Y MOTORCYCLE BUMPS INTO the back tire of the bike belonging to Bram Levine, the president of this shitty motorcycle club. The fucker cut me off, causing me to accidentally brake check the poor fuck behind me, earning me a bump from their fender and an exchange of insurance information.

It didn't take me long to have someone run the plate on the bike and get the name and address of this prick and his little club.

I'm tempted to push his bike over and put a bullet in anyone who dares say anything about it, but what I have planned will be more fun.

I swing my leg over my bike and push toward the party. My nose wrinkles at the smell of sweat, weed, and dirt. I've perfected the art of blending in; nobody ever notices my shadow that lies beside everyone.

A soft scent catches my attention, forcing me to pause in the doorway. It smells beautiful and alluring and has me turning my head, trying to gage where it is coming from. My shoulder is rubbed and I'm pushed backwards out of the doorway. This tiny, curvy bombshell pushes me out of the way, tossing her long hair behind her shoulder, unaware of who she just pushed to the side.

Each step she takes, her face displays disapproval, her nose tilted with annoyance. I'm captivated with the way her hips sway as she walks in like a queen reigning over her people. She has a grace to her that, while she may be forcefully pushing people out of her way, allows her to get away with it with style and finesse.

I follow her through the house, intrigued. Her cheeks flush when she sees a girl on her knees between the vice prez's legs. She pretends not to look but her eyes fall back to the girl giving head.

A strange magnetic sensation ripples through me as I watch her look innocent and flustered with the act. My heart taps twice, reminding me I have one.

She continues her mission and walks into the same office I was planning on entering. She swings the door open like she owns the place. I'm loving this sassy vibe she has going on. I wonder if she wants to kill the president like I do. Bram Levine rules with an iron fist and there's no exception for his daughter.

She has to be Sienna Levine. *Interesting.*

The door slams in my face and I'm reminded I need to stay on the sidelines. Bram can wait. My interest in ending him is gone, saving his life for now.

It doesn't take long for the door to swing back open and her eyes shine with unshed tears before she quickly schools her features.

I'm graced with that wonderful scent of hers again. It's the most intoxicating thing I've ever smelled. I follow on the heels of her, uncaring about anything. She continues to push everyone out of her way and I step from behind, trying to help make a path for her.

Her head stays focused on the ground as I part the crowd for her until she increases her speed, running right into me.

Her soft flesh bounces against mine and I turn to stare down at the angel trying to shove me to the side. Her body is soft, her hands flat on my chest. My hands tingle, wanting to grab hold of her waist, but I can't move, soaking up the moment.

She doesn't bother looking up and in slow motion, I watch as she lifts her foot and pushes down with all her might. So, this is Sienna Levine, daughter of the president, Bram Levine. I'd say she's more like a black angel instead of the golden halo type her father makes her out to be.

I watch her with interest and chuckle when I see a frown forming on her perfect skin. Her lips twist and she side steps me. I look ahead, toward the office she came from, and what should be my next destination, but I'll deal with that later now that she has side tracked me.

"Move, asshole." She raises her foot and stomps down on mine as hard as she can. At no time does she raise her face to look at mine, as if the angel she is, is afraid to look the devil in the eye.

Turning, I follow her at a distance. The white flesh dipping out of the bottom of her shorts draws my eyes with each step she takes. Her shirt is tight around her bust, curving in all the right places along her torso. I pull out my vape and take a drag while enthralled with Sienna. The feeling is consuming and overwhelming, as I've never felt this type of pull to anything but death before.

Goosebumps scatter on my arms and I know this one night won't be enough. I take another drag holding the raspberry vapor in my lungs for a long second before I blow it out to stop myself from going to her. She storms out of the club into the darkness of the night. Nothing good ever happens on the darkest of nights.

In the dark, she's digging a path with the way she's pacing back and forth while mumbling who knows what to herself. Out of the corner of my eye, I watch the dickwad vice prez step out to look vindictively at Sienna's gorgeous self. The man is a monster like her father. Neither one of them deserve her. The atmosphere becomes eerily static as I watch two prospects ordered to do something. They stalk Sienna like a caged animal and she has no idea. My hand grips my vape with more force than I intend. I already know if they touch her in any way, I'll kill them.

The feeling overwhelms me. Taking another drag, there's a huge part of me that wants them to do as I suspect. I'm going to enjoy torturing them. My feet shuffle as I get antsy, yet the normal, regular beat of my heart stays steady even as the cords in my neck tense at the thought of anyone putting their hands on her. It's the strangest sensation.

When I first came here, I thought I'd blow off some steam by killing Bram. I never imagined I would spiral into wanting to kill for someone.

The two prospects are a few yards from her. She's still pacing, oblivious of her surroundings. She's too comfortable here, believing her father will save her from everything.

The men stand behind her now, glancing at their boss, looking for cues to how they should be responding. He gives them a nod and they race toward her. One scoops her up, tossing her over their shoulder, while the other stays close. They drop her in the swamp muck at the far back of the property before the forest begins.

My vape cracks under the pressure of my grip as I'm forced to watch the club humiliate her by tossing her into the swampy goo at the end of the property. They all laugh, thinking they're the indispensable ones.

Wrong.

I've never felt I needed a moral compass before, but this girl here has me wanting to do right by her. The need to protect her forces the air out of my lungs like I've been kicked by a horse.

I study every face, knowing each of their times are up for laughing at what's mine. The air crackles with the new need to draw blood.

The smell coming off the dirt reminds me of my younger years on the pig farm with my brother Romeo. Back when he was still chasing those sinful kisses from his now wife.

Each of her screams for help gathers more attention from the rowdy crowd. I time how long it takes; each of them will live that many hours while wishing they were dead.

No one touches what's mine.

Mine? Where the fuck did that come from? *No, my toy.* My vape breaks under the pressure of my fingers and I toss it to the ground. My feet stay frozen, no one even aware I'm here. They will all pay.

I don't normally go out of my way to do a job to help someone, because I don't believe in giving anything for free. Me killing everyone would be a great service to the world.

More men join in on the laughing and I memorize their faces—ingrain them—so I never forget. That's the beauty of an eidetic memory. I'm able to recall everything like a photograph, including the mental picture I'm taking right now.

Sienna stands, flinging her hands to get the mud off, before walking out of the goo.

"You're a bunch of assholes," she shouts, stomping by me like I don't exist. We're not even a hand length away, and she's unaware of my stare. I close my eyes, inhaling her perfume.

There's something about this girl I can't let go of.

"Now, darling," the vice prez coos. "That's no way to speak to family. These are my men, and a woman won't be disrespectful to them."

Her eyes blaze, and I would love to know if she imagines killing him like I am.

"Fuck you," she seethes, stomping toward the front where all the vehicles are parked.

I stay on the outskirts, watching her get into her car, while quickly texting her license plate number to my guy. Within a second, I have her address and I'm heading toward her home.

She lives on the ground floor of a building. I watch as a light flicks on and she pours herself a glass of water, heading toward her bathroom. I'm tempted to explore while she's locked herself away, but force myself to refrain.

Oblivious that anyone can see into her apartment, she walks out of the shower thirty minutes later with a towel wrapped around her torso. She heads into her kitchen, pouring herself a glass of wine. I watch as she takes a large sip, closing her eyes, savoring the taste before she picks up her phone. Music instantly escapes the sliding patio door as I study each of her moves. She sways her hips, allowing the soft melodies to move her as she moves around the room drinking her wine. The way her curvy hips sway has me biting my knuckle. Damn, she's sexy.

It's almost two in the morning by the time she falls asleep. I let myself into her apartment, through her unlocked patio doors. My feet lead me to her room and I stand over her. My hands twitch to touch her, but I refrain. I don't know how light of a sleeper she is yet.

I watch her for an hour before I force myself to leave. My absence refuses to last long, and each night for the next month, I make this my routine. I come watch over my girl before I pluck each man who laughed at her off. One by one, they fall the same way. But I'm leaving her fiancé for last.

Chapter 2: Sienna

♥

A MONTH LATER

The only thing traditional about this wedding is that I'm wearing white. My dress is short, tight, going all the way to my neck, with a large circle missing in the back. My heels are bright red and three inches high, making my normal height of five feet one inches not stand out.

My fiancé stands in the so-called green space of the club. The club is a converted motel in the shape of a circle. The middle courtyard consists of dirt where they play with their bikes and drink, and it's here I get the *privilege* of being married.

My mother must be rolling over in her grave at the sight. I swallow the unease creeping up my throat as I watch my father trying to organize this pony show with a beer in his hand. The plastic blue cooler hinge creaks as it's opened, and I notice I'm the only person without a drink in their hand.

"Where the hell is Josh?" He's the prospect that took an online course, giving him the power to marry us. *Just great.* He's late, the reason we're all standing around looking like idiots.

I inspect my black nails, not caring when this starts. *The longer it takes, the better.* I watch the worried glances the others are giving each other. They're all thinking the same thing: He's not here, because he's dead. It wouldn't be the worst news I've heard.

The paper calls this shadow phantom a serial killer. All his victims are seen then disappear into thin air, always while they're around loved ones. It's rumored that it's The Butcher, a serial killer that threatened the area a decade ago. Somehow the paper hasn't said it's a hit against my father's motorcycle club, but we all know it to be true. Only our chapter is being targeted. It seems personal. Intimate. Vengeful.

"Did you just want to text me when he gets here, and I'll come back?" I toss out casually.

"I'm not giving you an opportunity to run," my father hisses into my ear. My fiancé must have something on him. It's the only explanation. I wish I was brave enough to run, but all I can think about are the stories of my mother. She tried to run, and now she's six feet under.

"Chad, go online and complete the course." My soon-to-be husband barks the order. *Dear Lord, who did I spite to deserve this?*

I cringe at the sound the plastic makes as I grab myself a beer and twist off the lid. I tilt my head back, allowing the bitter bubbles down my throat with one large gulp before I slip off my heels, curling my toes in the soft, warm dirt.

By the time Chad returns, I'm on my fourth beer and I'm the soberest one here. I don't bother placing my heels back on when my father calls everyone back to attention. I down my drink, tossing it into the pile gathering on the ground. It clunks and tings against the other bottles but doesn't break.

"Come on, woman," Jack calls, his voice grating on my nerves as I decide to pick up my bottle and place it on the table.

My steps are slow as I turn around, blowing out a breath that vibrates my lips. This is my future.

I roll my shoulders back as I walk toward this Chad guy—oh yeah, and my soon-to-be husband, too. My stomach rolls as the realization hits that I can't get out of this. My legs tremble with each step as I force myself closer.

"Let's get this over with," my fiancé growls. I don't know why he's grumpy. *I'm* the one marrying down, forfeiting true love and my future.

Chad begins, "Do you...?"

"Yes, I do. Yes, she does. The next part better be you announcing us husband and wife and telling me I can kiss my new wife."

My stomach drops with the realization I'm going to have to kiss him, and tonight...I...I can't go there yet.

"I pronounce you husband and wife. By the power—"

The sound of guns going off has everyone turning toward the parking lot, even though we can't see it from here.

"I have room number thirteen booked at the highway road side hotel. You better be in bed wearing something nice before I make my way there."

"You two need to sign here," Chad interrupts, shoving a pen in front of Jack before a pen is forced into my hand and Jack moves my hand to sign my name, after he signs his. My father quickly witnesses before they all go running into the club to get to the front.

A half hour later, the rev of engines fades down the road. Cautiously, I walk out. My car has two busted windows from gun fire. The hairs on the back of my neck stand on end when I realize this is the least of my worries. I'm the one thing I never wanted to be: an old lady.

I drive around, not wanting to go to the hotel. Who picks the number thirteen? I consider getting a twenty-four pack of beer and trying to drink them all before Jack gets there, but that's not my style.

When the street lights turn on, I make my way to the hotel. Jack's bike is parked out front. I'm pretty sure the only thing Jack loves is that bike. I'm tempted to push it over, but I don't. I need to keep the peace for at least tonight.

No one is at the front desk as I walk toward the so-called wedding suite. I take a deep breath, knowing there will be wrath to pay for me getting here after him. When I open the door, I'm not ready to see the scene displayed in front of me.

My fingers rake through my blonde hair. The tips of my nails scratching hard on my scalp. Red paints the normally-beige hotel room. *This is bad.* I take a slow step backward. My breathing is calm and even. Searching the room with my wide, green eyes, I take relief in that I haven't walked through anything coated in red. I take another step back. Once again, I'm double checking each step.

I curse at myself, knowing I already had a bad gut feeling about number thirteen. My hand rises to flick off the light, but pauses. The impulse to touch the blind to look outside is strong, but I refrain.

My fingers pull down at my sleeve, turning the handle. The hallway is bright. I want to pull my hood over my head, but that would stand out here. I know where every camera is, and I look in the opposite direction, keeping my face hidden even though they have my face on full display when I walked in here. The cameras might actually help me.

Buzzing attacks my leg, it pulses, unwelcome. It's not until I hit the now-rainy street that I pull my hood over my head, covering the tops of my eyes. My hand fishes for my phone and I see my father's name.

I'm done with this city and everything it represents. Coming to a busy corner, I'm conflicted about which way to go. My phone pulses again in my hand.

Let it go and leave, Sienna. Against my better judgment, I answer my phone. "Where the hell are you?" No, *hey I miss you.* Or *you're late and I'm worried.* Not even a greeting.

"You can't rush perfection."

He makes a sound and I think he just choked on his tongue. "Your husband is waiting. I can't save you from him, Sienna."

I roll my eyes as I cross the street. I don't know why I bother listening to him rambling on. I can have everything packed and ready to go. *I guess everyone deserves closure.*

"Goodbye, Dad."

This sets him off again, but I don't bother listening. I drop my phone into the closest garbage can and keep walking. It's time I get my life back. This time, I get to create the life I deserve.

Chapter 3: Copycat

I THINK MAXIMUS MANCINI would be proud of my work. I finished his list for him just the way he likes. He doesn't even know he's been a perfect teacher. As much as I would have loved taking out Jack Pierce, I didn't want to overstep my boundaries. I'll have to watch from the outside on this one.

Sienna Levine looks around in horror before a smirk raises her lips as realization dawns that her husband is dead. I can understand the fascination Max has with her.

She's a conundrum. I'm interested to see what Max ends up doing with her. It should be easy enough to lead them both to me.

Chapter 4: Max

♥

My head keeps swirling with the notion of a vacation, knowing I need to lie low for a while. Typically, when people talk about vacation, they're referring to the six feet under kind. That's not the definition I'm going for. I want to disappear with Sienna. It won't be long before she concludes she had to leave, too.

The problem is, when I see a person, all I can do is size them up and ponder the best way to dispose of them. It's second nature. Within a second, I know how I would kill them. My fingers tingle, wanting to become useful in the deadliest way, and I have to place my hands in my pockets and pinch my leg to stop myself from the act. It's hard to have self control. It's not like that with Sienna, though. Problem is, I can't stop seeing the panic in her gorgeous moss irises when she walked into the hotel room.

I round my car and head to my favorite place to dispose of my victims. This one isn't getting the regular treatment like the others. I had to get it over fast, too fast. The press is already writing daily stories about me, even though their claims are inaccurate. I'm not the one who has killed everyone on my list. Someone else has been doing it for me.

My thoughts reread the letter he sent me, word for word. It praises my work, calling me a legend. Telling me I'm the only one worthy of his letters. I've burned them all after I dusted for fingerprints. It was a dead end.

All I want is to pin my murders on someone. Bumping off a third of the motorcycle club was a little too much, even though it wasn't all me. That many kills in such a short period was overkill, literally, and now the cops are sniffing around. Knowing all of this, the beast from within couldn't stop, and now the pressure breathes down my neck, as this is the closest I've come to getting caught.

If a wannabe fan found me, I'm no longer invisible. It's what I've prided myself on. I could go anywhere and never be seen. The letters haunt me, not that I would ever tell anyone about them.

The rain pours down as I drop my last tarp into the incinerator before closing the heavy metal door and pressing the large red button labeled 'on'. The walls shake as it throttles to life before the heat is felt on my fingertips. This is definitely against code, but lucky for me, this plant was shut down a decade ago.

My whole life I've followed my father or brother. I've always been willing to do anything for them. It's how I earned the nickname The Butcher, but for the first time in my life, I want that name to be gone and get a fresh start.

If only I can come up with an idea to spin this, to make it look like an advantage to the *costa nostra*.

"FUCKING HELL, MAX. THEY'RE pinning this murder on The Butcher." My brother, Romeo, tosses the newspaper at me.

"It was me. You should read the online version. It's much better." My eyes stay on my phone while I eat my breakfast. It's the only meal guaranteed in my day. Shit goes sideways fast, then you're out for twenty-four hours cleaning up messes and problems.

"What about this one?" He tosses another paper. It makes a thud on the table.

I lean over, curious what this one could be. I burn most of my victims. I can't keep the smile off my face thinking about the ones I don't burn. There's always a reason. I leave them to highlight what a shitty person they are. I'm doing the world a favor.

"That's not mine," I respond, reaching for my coffee. For some reason, peanut butter mixed with jam and my coffee tastes like birthday cake. Each time I take a bite, and then have a sip of coffee, its flavor explodes in my mouth. It's my favorite combination. My eyes close as I savor the taste.

When I open my eyes again, I say, "I have an admirer." Referring to the copycat the article described.

Romeo is glaring down at me. He's so much more uptight now that he has children.

"They're calling you a fucking serial killer!" His neck strains under the anger he's trying to control.

I snort. "That's hardly the case."

A drop of water in my ear from my shower earlier catches my attention and I tip my head, trying to draw it out.

Romeo keeps on whining. "The fucking cops are sniffing around."

"I'm not a serial killer. I can't help if someone is trying to mimic me. We have a hundred enemies. It could be anyone."

"Maybe it's time you take things seriously in life."

I place my warm cup down and stand. I match my brother's gaze at eye level and lean into him. "I take my job very seriously. I have protected the Rossi sisters with my life more than once. Your wife's family. Not mine. You need someone handled, I do it. Never disrespect me again, brother."

I sit back down, but my breakfast is ruined. I can't enjoy it. If I can't savor its taste, what's the point of eating it?

"How about I lie low?" I soften my tone as an idea gains traction. "Let me disappear. A vacation of sorts."

Romeo's lips stay perfectly flat, giving no indication of what he's thinking.

"If I know where you are, everyone else will know. No one takes vacations, anyway," he scoffs.

"That's the thing. Not even you will know where I am. I'll come home when it's safe." I'm not sure if it's a lie. There's a possibility I'll never return.

I NEVER THOUGHT I'D live by an ocean, but I have to give Sienna credit, Oakport Beach is the perfect location. It's far from any city. Its police force is an inherited milestone. Generation after generation of the same family. Tourists haven't taken over, but there are enough new people coming into town that it's not weird.

I've rented a place out of town; a little cabin surrounded by trees. My closest neighbor is a boarded-up house that's seen better days. The same place Sienna has called multiple times regarding its rent. I have a little shed where I keep all of my knives and guns. I've reinforced its structure, and no one is getting in or out of it. I couldn't part without my tools. I still enjoy cleaning, polishing, and organizing them, even if they're not being used. This town would notice someone missing, unlike the city.

I'm like every other dude out there. Instead of puttering around in a garage with hammers and screwdrivers, I have other tools. The process is the same.

There's a crow that lives on my property. It would take me less than a minute to get rid of its nest, but I'm tuning a new leaf. No more killing for me.

The black bird caws then swoops down, standing near my laptop. My new university course went live yesterday. Once I complete it, I'll have my fourth honoree degree. I'm trying to think of what degree I want to do next. I need to do something with my free time.

A shriek demolishes the peace in my yard and my crow flies away. I'm moving through the trees before I can think. I'm like a bear catching a scent that he can't say no to. The shrieks keep coming, with a new sense of profoundness. Coming to the edge of the forest, I pause.

"Shoo!" Sienna is whipping her handbag around at a bobcat that's sizing her up. Her hair is a mess, with small pieces falling out of the elastic that holds the majority of it up. She's changed the color from blonde to a light chocolate brown.

I pull the small hunting knife from around my ankle and wonder if I could wrestle with the big cat and make it out alive. The thought sends a thrill down my spine before I realize what I'm attempting. No more killing. Not even wild animals that deserve it.

I watch as her hands shake, and each time she screams, her eyes widen. My eyes trail down her body, loving the fact I could easily dominate her. An image of her tied up at my mercy flashes through my mind.

I take slow steps backward, out of view. I want Sienna and me to meet on my terms once I think an introduction is necessary.

Sienna manages to open her car door and blares the horn before the wild cat decides to leave. He turns, looking like she's too much trouble to deal with at the moment.

"That's right, and don't come back!" she yells at the departing animal like it was her bravery that sent it away. She's an adorable, feisty, curvy, little thing. Her right arm is covered in what looks like intricate tattoos. I guarantee she has a full sleeve.

She can't be much taller than five feet. She attempts to pull her thick light brown hair back into a bun on her head by shoving the pieces under a fluffy elastic thing. Once the bobcat is out of view, she turns her back to the trees, her shoulders visibly relaxing.

I watch, mesmerized, as she brings one suitcase out of the back of her car. Huffing and puffing, she drags it through the dirt. Its heavy size leaves a grooved trail in the dirt and each step protests with a creak against its weight. The deck bangs as she drops her luggage on each decrepit step. She gets to the last step and her foot falls through the rotting wood. A scream, followed by another trail of long-winded curses, leave her mouth.

I have to place my hand on the tree to stop me from running to her aid. My thumb and forefinger rub at my bottom lip. My body shifts, trying to get a better look while concealing my position.

A twig breaks and her attention snaps in my direction. I fall to the ground, not wanting to be found. It's not time for introductions yet.

Chapter 5: Sienna

♥

WHO KNEW SMALL TOWNS were so boring? There's nothing to do but go to church. That's how I find myself at a Sunday barbeque outside a church with its congregation.

Heat creeps over me and I have that familiar sensation that I'm being watched. Ever since the so-called engagement party, I can't shake this feeling. It doesn't just occur in the darkness of the night, but during the day, too. It's like I have a second shadow that follows me everywhere.

"How are you liking Oakport Beach?" I jump at the question that pulls me out of my thoughts. The preacher's daughter, Haven, is looking at me expectantly for a response. She's about my age, maybe a little older. Mid twenties.

I purposely shoved a cookie in my mouth, hoping to squirm away from their questions, but she and her best friend, Frankie, are staring at me, waiting for an answer. Both women are too nice for their own good, but I appreciate it. I nod, raising a finger, and visibly swallow.

"Everyone is so friendly; it's hard not to love." My voice rises slightly at my lie. These women are too nice to lie to, but I think they would take it personally if I said I hated the town.

Everyone wants to get to know you. I can't blend in by trying to stay hidden. People stop by my abandoned little home trying to give me food or offer their skill to help out. What this town does have? Isolation from the rest of the world. No major newspaper's line counters; everyone reads the small local press. Every business has the name Crash in it somewhere. People believe in getting to know you rather than social media stalk you. They also believe anything you tell them.

"You should join our choir," Haven suggests, her eyes lighting up with the idea.

"Or our book club," Frankie adds, nodding her head up and down repeatedly. "Really, we just drink wine, and bring the book we were supposed to read, but never get around to talking about it."

I'm trying to think what I would have in common with these ladies. They look like they grew up in loving, supportive homes.

I, on the other hand, wouldn't even know what that looked like if it hit me over the head. My mom was an old lady to another member of my father's MC, then she became his. I was four when she decided she wanted to leave my father. I watched him shoot her in our driveway as she packed me and our stuff in a car. The whole reason why she was still outside when he roared up on his bike was because I forgot my favorite stuffy and she went back to get it. No one runs away and lives to talk about it. It's why I married when my father told me, and now it's the reason I'm hiding in this small town of Oakport Beach.

"I just might do both." I smile. The heat of unknown eyes is still felt and I cast my gaze around the perfect setting used for movies and not real life.

Haven touches my arm and I involuntarily flinch. Both girls catch it but are too sweet to say anything. I look down at my tattoo-free skin. It's all a lie. Special makeup covers my markings. I hate to cover them, but it's a requirement to stay low in this type of town.

"You know my cousin, Crash, is looking for someone to help answer phones for him," Frankie says out of nowhere. "If you need a job, I could put in a good word."

Crash. That's why everything is named that around here. "I would love that." Again, another lie. But I need a job or people will start asking questions.

My arms itch with all the lies I'm spinning. "I should get going. I have a lot of work to get done on the house."

"If you ever want company, we can come and help," Haven offers.

"I appreciate that. It might come sooner than you think."

My eyes land on a tall man. His shoulders slouch like he's trying to look shorter. Going by his bulky size, he looks like he does a lot of physical work. I connect eyes with him briefly and my stomach flip-flops. His eyes are hard. I recognize them because similar eyes stare back at me in the mirror. He doesn't smile or grin, instead, his eyes drop to the mini goat he's leading with a leash. His glasses fall down his nose, and for a second, I swear I see a patch of color under his shirt trying to poke out. That's my old life. This man looks to be nothing but a kind nerd helping out.

"That's Max," Frankie replies, not being asked. "Actually, I think you two live near each other."

"He's super friendly," Haven hastily adds. I wonder if she thinks he looks like a hot, older geek. "He's been helping my dad around the church."

I nod. Trying not to watch him too closely, and force myself to give the ladies my attention back. *He's nothing but another church-loving person to occupy this town.* I almost laugh at myself for making him out to have tattoos. That was my old life, and yet, the need to escape becomes stronger. What if the MC has someone looking for me? He could look like one of them. If you ditch the glasses, straighten his posture and paint his skin...*stop*!

Disappointment builds in my gut and I realize this town is growing on me and I want to stay, for at least a little bit. I glance over at the man, seeing him trip over a goat. He obviously hasn't grown into his length. My paranoia has to stop. No one knows I'm here. I've never considered any place home, and part of me wanted this to be it.

"Apparently, he transferred here from Kansas. He came with glowing references from his previous church," Haven tells us.

Yup, not from the MC.

"I need to work on my renovations. Thanks for having me." I step away, needing the safety of my home.

I'VE KEPT MY WINDOWS boarded up. It makes me feel safer. I've replaced the deck boards that have rotted with new ones. Now I'm attempting to make the inside more comfortable. I've painted the main room a bright yellow. It brightens up the place and I notice no natural light streaming through.

Each time I hear the sound of crumbling rock and dirt crackling from the weight of a vehicle, my ears perk up, listening to see if they're turning into my long, secluded driveway. The sound from the road stops and it has me walking outside. I can see a car stopped at the top, and my pulse begins to race.

My eyes search the forest. I hadn't known there was another house near mine. I should have done a better job searching it out. I wonder if he would be able to hear me scream. My gaze flicks back to the unmoving car.

My fingers twitch, wanting to go inside to grab a weapon, but I don't want anyone to sneak up on me. After a few moments, the car drives away. It's only then I'm able to take a deep breath.

I place my bear spray and knife in my purse and decide to go back into town. I'll be safer there for now. I lace up my hiking boots. Each day I've been trying to get the lay of the land by walking through the heavily-forested area until it thins out to where the start of town is.

A BELL ABOVE MY head rings as I step into the local pub. It's one of the few places without the Crash name.

"Take a seat where you want," a male's voice calls out as I walk toward the long counter of the bar. A low growl catches my attention, pulling my eyes down to see a large German Shepherd lying on the ground, showing its teeth at me.

"Don't take him personally. That means he likes you." The bartender tosses a treat up and the dog stops paying attention to me. It sits up, catching the treat in his large jaws.

"Shouldn't the guard dog be outside?" I raise my brow as I take a seat.

"He guards the counter when I have to run to the back. It's not an issue during the day, but if I leave this unattended at night, it'll be free beer for everyone."

"What if someone is allergic?" I question.

He shrugs. "Then I guess they suck it up or they don't come in. I haven't had any complaints yet. Did you want to put one in?" He gives me a smirk and I laugh.

"You might have to loan him to me when I walk home tonight."

"I was just about to offer that, he's all yours when you leave. I'm Elliot Eldrige, by the way." He extends his hand over the counter.

"Sienna." I shake his hand, looking around. "Why is this bar one of the few places not to have the name Crash in it?"

He lets out a booming, deep laugh. "I just bought this place and had the same question when I moved to town. My only answer is because Crash Jennings doesn't own it." He raises his hands in front of us and I can't help but think he looks quite charming. "What can I get you?"

"Whatever you have on tap."

He grabs a frosted glass. "A beer girl. You'll fit in alright here."

I look around the worn place and can't help but think it reminds me of home. "When do you get busy?"

He slides my drink over to me and places his elbow on the counter. "It's Sunday. You'll be my only customer."

"Their loss is my gain," I flirt. Just as I say it, the hair on my arm rises. My head turns toward the door and the tall nerdy guy from earlier walks in with a thick textbook in his hands.

"Looks like there will be the two of you now," Elliot says, grabbing another glass.

I watch as the stranger sets his book on the counter and takes out a pad of paper with writing already on it. Elliot pours him a drink without a word being spoken. My first assessment was right. He's a nerd through and through.

"Aren't you a little old to be studying for school?"

His body pauses and it takes a second for him to raise his stormy dark-blue eyes to me. It reminds me of a summer storm that catches everyone off guard with its power. My heart stills for a moment when his eyes meet mine.

He's bulkier than I assessed from before. Under his long-sleeved shirt, muscles protrude and stretch the material out, displaying his toned body. He looks like he could be a bodyguard or an enforcer. I imagine the person who finds me will look a lot like him.

I have to force my eyes down and study my drink before I take a sip. My paranoia is getting the best of me. I thought this would stop once I settled in.

When I look back, he's already forgotten about me. His attention is on the book in front of him. It has me wanting to talk to him. My heart beats a little faster. I stand, moving two seats closer.

"You're new to town," I state, taking another sip of my drink. My thumb rubs at the wet sweat of the glass.

"Not as new as you." His voice is deep and gravely. It's like one of those movie narrators. My stomach flutters upon hearing it.

This time he takes his time looking me over. There's something about him that I can't put my finger on. I want to break the silence by asking a question, but that would lead to him asking me questions. He leans on his arms on the counter, his forearms showcasing his muscle.

It looks like he might say something, but then he positions his body so that his textbook becomes the center of his attention once again.

Everyone but this guy is friendly. The rest of the town goes out of their way to make sure I feel at home, but not him. Is that what's bothering me?

For the rest of the night, we sit in silence, not exchanging a word as I eat my dinner. It reminds me of all the times I had to eat by myself at home. *At least I was able to have a delicious meal.* It was like something you would get at home, and not some local pub. I have a slight buzz happening that relaxes me.

"I'll get the bill, please," I call out because, other than Max, I don't see anyone else. I can see why this guy thinks he needs a guard dog.

The dog barks, causing me to jump, and the bartender re-emerges. "Sorry, I was doing inventory. Are you off for the night?" Elliot asks.

"Yeah, it's time I walk my ass back home."

"It's dark out, take Princess with you." The dog sits up, her ears perking at her name.

"That's kind, but I'm safe to walk alone."

Elliot is already gathering the leash from the wall on the other side and the dog's tail is wagging. "I insist. Just tie him up outside when you get home and I'll get him once I close down for the night. He's a great guard dog. You just have to tell him to attack and he will on command."

"Your dog is a him?"

The bartender lifts a brow, not answering.

"Cool." I was just making sure I heard right.

I glance over at Max to gauge his attention, but he's not listening to our conversation.

I'm left with no choice as I'm handed a leash with a dog on the other end of it. The dog curls his lips at me. I'm not sure if it's in a smile or trying to show me his teeth. Dogs, as a general rule, don't like me. This one seems to be on board with that assessment.

I begin walking out before I realize I haven't said thank you or my address. "Thank you, but how do you know where I live?" Once again, the hairs on my arm shoot up.

"Small town. There are no secrets here."

I nod and Princess follows me out with no problem. The dog is slow, keeping my speed down. I wasn't expecting the night to be darker than I'm used to. There are no street lights as I leave the main street, heading toward my little cabin.

The slight incline has Princess stopping to lie down. We still have five minutes to go, so I pull on his leash. He has to be close to a hundred pounds, there's no way I can carry him.

"Come on, get up," I try to coax him with my sweetest voice.

"I thought you hated dogs..." A deep voice comes out of nowhere and my eyes dart around as I move in a circle. It takes my eyes a few seconds to see a hooded figure with my father's motorcycle club patch faded on the clothing. If I wasn't so familiar with the logo, I would have missed it. A knife is held in his hand, and it takes me a moment before recognition settles in. Ben, my dead husband's son, stands before me, and I know he never leaves home without a gun.

"What do you want?" My voice is steady but I can feel the fight my body is having trying not to tremble. He's here to bring me home, dead or alive.

His finger shakes in my direction. "It's funny how my father ends up dead the same night you leave town. Coincidence? I think not." He steps closer to me. Princess is still lying on the ground. *Worst guard dog ever.*

My hand is pulling on the leash with each backward step I take until I can't go any further. I look around for an escape route, already knowing he could easily catch me. My heart pounds double time with the realization that I'm fucked. Ben has over a hundred pounds of muscle on me; he could immobilize me within seconds. The doubling of my heart spikes radically when I watch the evil gleam of his eye, knowing he has won. I'm going to die and no one will ever find my body, just like my mother. Her casket was empty when it was lowered into the ground.

My eyes stay trained to the knife he wields in his hand. "Good news. Since you were my father's, you get to be my old lady when I bring you home alive."

"If I had known, I would have never run." I try to fix a flirtatious vibe to my voice, but it comes out shaky.

"You okay, Sienna?" The deep voice has Ben pausing, the same moment the clouds roll over the moon, taking all the light with it. We stand in the middle of nowhere in the pitch black. I tug harder at Princess, not recognizing the new voice.

In the distance, lightning flashes, illuminating another hooded figure, with a textbook, between me and Ben. Blackness takes over once again and I jump at the crack of thunder.

The flash of the sky shows Max dropping his book to the ground without care. Great, now I'm going to have his death on my conscience too. Maybe Ben will kill me first so I don't have to know.

A knife replaces the book in an instant and Ben lunges at Max. I'm frozen, my voice unable to make a sound. I'm completely locked in as my muscles turn to stone and panic ripples through me. I hate this feeling. I've worked hard to never be placed in this position again.

Max is swift, his moves looking effortless. That nerdy persona he had going disappears as something entirely different emerges. His shirt is slashed, showing a chest of beautiful artwork. It's not long before Max has Ben in a sleeper hold.

Sharp tiny pin pricks are felt over my skin as my muscles loosen. "Attack," my voice comes out strong, as if it was never locked away. Princess jumps up, biting Ben's leg and refuses to let go.

Chapter 6: Max

I CAN'T CONCENTRATE ON the book spread out on the bar counter because Sienna's perfume keeps wafting over to me. My fingers curl around the pages as I force myself not to stare at her in the seat next to me. Each time she tries to gain my attention, my dick strains in my pants.

She's the first person I've encountered where the first thing I haven't thought about is which artery I'd choose if I had to slash one. Instead, my attention is on the quick pulse of her neck, and I wonder what it would feel like under my lips.

When she leaves the tavern to walk home, I tell myself I'm only making sure she gets there okay. I'm not stalking her. If anything, I'm protecting her. What if she crosses another bobcat?

The night is dark without the artificial glow of street lamps. The moon reflects off the water nearby, but does little to light a path. I see him approach her before she does. My pulse speeds up, excitement builds in my veins. My muscles act on memory when the man threatens her with a knife, and I revert back into my old self. I act on impulse, not remembering any of my moves until I'm left staring at her wide eyes and the man is in a choke hold. If I don't let go in the next few seconds, he will die.

Fuck. I'm scaring the shit out of her.

"Attack," she yells. I wait for the dog to take a chunk out of me. Instead, he goes for the man I'm holding. It's enough to snap me out of it and I drop the guy like he's burned me.

My hand swipes through my hair. The dog still hasn't taken his teeth out of the attacker's leg.

I take the other end of the leash. "Relax," I demand, and the dog releases his hold, returning to Sienna.

Her body is still and she leans away from me. I keep my eyes on her, waiting to see if she's going to make a run for it. My body matches her tenseness, because I'm anticipating this guy getting up and trying to kill one of us.

"Are you hurt?" I keep my voice low and try to soften it as much as possible. It sounds strange hearing me like this.

"No." I have to strain my ears to hear her.

Moaning has both our eyes looking down. "Sienna, when I get my hands on you—"

My jaw grinds at the tone he takes. I want to put him out of his misery for disrespecting her.

I kick him in the stomach, my anger getting the best of me. "When you address her, I expect you to do it politely."

He groans and attempts to stand. "She's a fucking whore. Don't waste your time on her."

I step into him and punch him in the face, sending his sorry ass back to the gravel. "If I have to remind you a second time..." I pause as I'm about to tell him I plan to bury him six feet under, but I can't do that with Sienna in my presence.

I crouch down, balancing on my heels, trying to keep my voice calm and steady. "Leave town and don't come back."

She steps to me when I stand, and I place a protective arm around her.

My hand tingles, wanting to finish him off. If he's still in town by morning, I'll get rid of him. I'm getting rusty; it will be good to keep up my skills. What if my brother needs me and I forget how to do my job? Maybe I'll track him down before dawn.

Who am I kidding? I'm killing the guy no matter what.

Sienna is frozen to my side, her eyes glued on the asshole. I hate it. "He's bleeding a lot. Is he going to be alright?" I glance down at her, hating the way her voice sounds concerned.

"Do you want him to be alright?" I ask, studying her facial expressions, but the darkness makes it hard, and it's not like I've ever been great at reading emotions.

"If I say no, I'm a horrible person, right?"

I can't help the smirk that grows on my face, but I quickly remove it.

"It's natural to want pain delivered to an attacker."

"Him being alive is going to cause more problems," she mumbles.

I want to show her who I really am. I would love to place a dagger in his heart and have her watch, but she's not ready yet, and clearly not thinking straight. Her trembling hand still holds the dog's leash as she stares down at the asshole.

I pick Sienna up, bridal style, and walk toward my place. She squirms in my hold but I refuse to let go of her. She's the only thing stopping me from finishing the job right now. My back molars grind as I contemplate how he'll lose his life.

"You're kind of hurting me." Her sweet voice ripples over my skin. I look down and I have her bicep gripped in my hand and my other hand is holding her ankle.

I clear my throat, my voice gruff. "Sorry." I loosen my hold while keeping my pace.

"I can walk. You came in time. He didn't hurt me." Her soft, warm hand cups the bottom side of my face. No woman has ever touched me so delicately. It has me wanting to tie her up.

"You're staying with me tonight," I grunt.

She wiggles in my arms again, her movements sending a shock wave to my cock, waking it up.

"You don't have to go out of your way. I can take care of myself." I glance down at her. This girl is the definition of someone who needs to be protected. Otherwise, the wrong people will take advantage.

"Seriously, I'm fine. Let me down." Princess growls at me with her tone and, reluctantly, I let her down.

"This way." I tilt my head in the direction.

"The bartender is coming to my house to get Princess and the whole place is boarded up. I'll be fine, but I appreciate you walking me back."

"No." She steps back at my forceful tone. Shit. I'm going to scare her away. I soften my voice. "What I mean is. I'd like you to think about it."

"I'm used to taking care of myself, and I know nothing about you."

"Ask anyone around. They'll all tell you about my boring upbringing. If it makes you comfortable, you can let someone know where you are. Maybe Haven or Frankie? I saw you talking to them at church today. Or I can drop you off at one of their houses."

I hate the idea of her anywhere but with me, yet it would give me more time to deal with the mystery man.

"If I'm not stressing, neither should you." She looks incredibly serious. I want to kiss that frown off her lips.

"Fine, but I want you to know that I'm a gentleman through and through." *Said no one ever before…*

She seems to believe me and we continue to walk to her cabin. There's an awkward silence when we reach her doorstep.

"Let me make you a tea or warm milk, then I'll be on my way."

She thinks about my request, then nods. "Okay, thank you."

Sienna is wound up, and if I don't do something about it, she'll never fall asleep. Each tick of the clock is another reminder that Ben is getting a farther head start. I place a sleeping pill in her water and have her drink it. Within half an hour, she's sleeping on her couch.

I cradle her small body in my arms and place her in her bed. I debate if I should put her into something more comfortable. *That might scare her off*. Fighting the urge to make her more comfortable, I pull the covers over her and turn off the lights.

Now it's my time to play. The anticipation of it has me overly excited. I set up my motion detectors and silent alarms. Sienna's beautiful face stays on the camera of my phone as I head out into the night.

Chapter 7: Sienna

♥

LIGHT SEEPS THROUGH MY closed eyes, and my lashes slowly flutter open. It takes me a second to recognize my surroundings. The confusion happens more than I would like to admit. I try to remember how I got in my bed, but my mind is blank. I recall fighting to keep my eyes open, but that's about it. I'm still fully clothed, which is nothing out of the ordinary. I like falling asleep in my clothes. It makes it easier to wake up and go if I have to.

I jolt upright when I remember Max being in my house. *Did he put me in my bed?* It's driving me crazy that I can't remember. Never mind that the MC will be coming for me once Ben runs back and tells everyone where I am. *I have to leave.* I frantically go to my dresser, tossing my limited belongings into my suitcase. A few items land outside my target while others land part way in, before the slight melody of classical music strums its ways between the walls and me.

Pausing, I try to gauge where it's coming from before shoving the clothes inside and zipping it up. My hand pulls on the handle, bringing it to my living room before letting go. That soft sound has me curiously walking toward the melody, its invisible notes pulling me along to open my front door. The door is locked and I breathe a sigh of relief. I had to have put myself to bed.

Trying not to make a sound, I turn the handle and step out. Max is writing equations on a small white board, his head not looking up as I step outside. I stand there, leaning against my door, taking all of him in. He's incredibly sexy with his messy, wet hair and his forehead scrunched in concentration. His button-up shirt is open, displaying his chiseled torso. My eyes refuse to look away as I gawk at him for a moment or two before I kick myself for openly checking him out.

"Is studying the only thing you do for fun?" I ask, stepping closer to him.

He laughs. "It helps me focus my mind. Otherwise, I get fixated on stuff." He has this boyish smile that has my heart fluttering.

"Like you're fixated on that board?"

He considers my comment. "I guess, but it also helps to keep my mind from wandering to a hundred different things."

I take a seat on the stairs of my porch, looking out into the gorgeous treed area. The soft music is calming, coaxing my muscles to relax, and the sun warms me.

"Thank you for last night," I say quietly, not making eye contact.

The crunch of the gravel has our heads lifting to the sound. A police car slowly drives down the driveway. My heart rate spikes, its natural reaction to authorities, even though I have no reason for it. Cops always do that for me. I swipe my clammy palms over my pants.

The officer steps out of the car and takes off his hat. "Sorry to bother you, Sienna and Max." I don't know how he knows my name, other than this is a small town.

"I just wanted to come up here and let you know there was an animal attack in these parts last night." The cop looks around the area, concerned etched across his face. "Seems to have been a tourist hiking by themselves. Do you recognize this man? We're trying to identify him." The cop holds up a photo of Ben.

Max steps closer. "Can't say I've seen him before, sorry. Just the other day, I had to scare a bobcat off my deck," he replies. I watch as Max shows no signs that we know the man in the picture.

"So did I. I had to honk my horn to get it to leave," I confirm.

My heart is hammering my ribs. My short fingernails scrape against my palm as I look for an easy exit to run toward.

"If you're walking alone out here, make sure to carry bear spray on ya, Sienna," the officer lectures, his chest expanding. He hooks his one hand on his belt, drawing my eyes to the gun holster attached to him. My eyes draw back up and I look at his badge: Clayton McCain.

"Will the man be alright?" I ask, forcing worry into my tone.

"No ma'am. Unfortunately, he didn't make it. We're trying to find his next of kin."

Relief floods my core and I nod, not saying any more.

"Have a good day now." Officer McCain walks back to his car and reverses out of the property.

I take a seat back on my porch, my legs unable to hold me up. Out of the corner of my eye, Max goes back to the problem he was working on before I came out.

We sit in silence, my mind whirling with immense relief. I would have thought silence would be uncomfortable, but it's not. I sneak a glance at Max. Why did he lie? The question circles around in my head for long minutes until I blurt out, "Why did you lie?"

"I figured you wouldn't want to have this town all up in your business." He shrugs, but his eyes stay on mine. It's unnerving and feels as if he'd be able to dig up everything I'm trying to hide if he worked hard enough.

"I appreciate that. But you didn't have to."

"I know that. I did it for you," he says with sincerity.

My ears whoosh at the extra blood pumping through my veins. Anxiety is a bitch. I'd love to kick her down to the curb and walk right over her. I don't trust men. It's never worked out in my favor before.

Chapter 8: Max

♥

"I HAVE A JOB for you," my brother, Romeo, the Don of the Mancini family says over the phone.

"How the hell are you calling me?" No one is supposed to have this number. "Now I have to get a new burner phone," I complain, cleaning up the mess my latest victim made in my shed.

My veins still thrum from my kill. I should have known better; a person like me can't just quit. It's like trying not to breathe, but it's the oxygen that keeps you surviving.

After I made sure Sienna wasn't too shook up from the night before, I went out to find my next trophy. This one was less of a saint than Ben. Blood still clings to the knife I used. I don't think I can get away with an animal attack like before. Deeply inhaling my surroundings, the metallic scent calms my nerves. I want to have this feeling every day. The task of trying to find a place to burn the evidence won't be easy. I kick myself for acting impulsively and not figuring this step out first.

"Did you not hear what I said? I have a job. I thought you would be jumping at the chance."

My mind is cluttered while I wipe my weapon clean with a cloth. She almost had a glimpse of the monster that lurks just beneath the surface. I blow out a breath. It's too dangerous to get close. She's already seen that I've lied for her. I've done too much. I need to keep my distance like I had before.

But the image of her in her bed has my imagination running wild. I bite my knuckle, wishing I could have my way with her. She would look so pretty with her skin pink and her hands tied up the way I like.

"Are you listening to me?" Romeo hollers on the other end of the phone.

"Yeah, yeah, tell me the job."

It doesn't escape my attention that I allowed her to touch my face. That never happens. I could lose my self-control in a split second. It's a hazard of the occupation, and while I love what I do, it sickens me to think I could hurt someone I love. I can never allow myself to come undone around anyone.

"Sienna Levine." The only thing I hear is her name. My heart stills.

"I don't kill women. What the fuck, Romeo?"

"I know, I know," he tries to placate me. "I thought maybe you might be getting desperate. It's good money. Apparently, she killed her husband on their wedding night. The MC from a few cities over is in an uproar and is going under some civil war between members. They asked and I said I'd get back to them. We don't need the money, I'm happy to say no."

"Wait." *Fuck me.* If I don't accept, someone will be after her. It's hard to keep her safe from unknown enemies.

"I'll do it, but make sure they know the process. I leave no evidence."

"I explained that, and they weren't thrilled, but said okay because of your reputation."

"Send over the details and I'll get on it." I hang up; looking over all the tarps I use to keep the wood evidence free.

T HE NEXT DAY, I walk into the police station with my friendly smile. I hate interacting with people, but society requires it. If I want to blend in, this small town requires me to go out of my comfort zone.

"Clayton!" I greet officer McCain.

I hated the way he looked at Sienna and the concern that was etched into his face. It doesn't sit well with me. It's why I'm here to make a friend out of him.

He gives me a nod and raises his finger while he has a phone glued to his ear before he goes behind a wall. I look around the small station. Honestly, this place is a wet dream for guys like me. I don't think they have any sort of system for big crimes. Maybe it's time I place down some temporary roots. I could start a car wash. I haven't seen one here, and specialize it to also include animals to be washed. It's a crazy enough idea that this town would go insane over it, and a perfect way to launder money.

I walk over to a cork board and see a missing person board. A few hikers, a lot of indigenous women. Where do these people go? Stupid question. *I know what I would do.* I'd never mentioned it to anyone before, but I once donated a third of my wages to find missing people.

Before I can think further into that thought, a blonde woman's smile catches my attention from the board and I happen to know she's no longer blonde, but brunette...Sienna. Looking over my shoulder, I make sure no one is around. I lift the push pin and take the missing person's picture off, folding it before I slip it in my back pocket.

"What can I help you with?" McCain's voice rounds the corner as I turn around.

"Need a lunch break?" I ask. You know the saying, keep your friends close, but your enemies closer.

He snaps his fingers. "I would love to, but I just got a call and have to head out."

I raise my hands. "No problem. Another time."

Walking out of the station, I take a quick glance around, spotting Sienna down the street. She's just entering the local grocery store. I can't seem to let this girl go. Something about her has me wanting to know more about her. I can't help myself and follow her into the store.

A distinct skunk smell catches my attention and I notice more people are looking around to see where it's coming from. Sienna pivots her direction and stalls when she sees me a few feet behind her. Her eyes dart around and my eyes land on her lips. An unwelcome hint of desire rushes through my body. I cautiously step closer, her eyes widening a fraction as she looks like she wants to find the nearest exit. There's clear avoidance in her expression, there's no missing the fact that she didn't want to see me.

Disappointment clings to my nerves, an odd feeling. My gaze leaves her face, going to her cart. It's lined with boxes of douche and cans of tomato juice. An odd combination.

"Having a party tonight?" I joke, the tension radiating from the two of us swirling around. Her cheeks grow pink, the flush spreading all the way to the tips of her ears. She's fucking adorable. Like a stray pussy cat I want to take in and tame.

That skunk smell assaults my nostrils and I force myself to try not to breathe too hard. I hate mouth breathers, and here I am doing it. It's awful. I swear I can taste the smell. "Does this store always smell like this?" My nose wrinkles while I look around for the cause.

Her lips tighten, another hammer to my chest is felt. *What the hell is wrong with me?*

She mumbles something I can't catch, and I step closer. The smell must be coming from behind her. "I think it's behind you," I say.

"It's me." Her voice is slightly louder. This time I take in her appearance. Her chest is the same pink that matches her cheeks. She looks more embarrassed than anything.

"How the hell is that you?" I ask without thinking of filtering my word choice. She visibly flinches, and we get a few looks.

Her wide gaze flicks back to me and her eyes darken with a rawness I don't expect. My spine tingles, hearing desperation in her voice, and fuck me. It has me wanting to do bad, pleasurable things to her, even with the stench clouding around us.

"It's skunk. I was out when a bobcat came into my yard and I wasn't looking where I was going because I was trying to get out of the way. Then *bam*! A skunk is in front of me with its tail lifted and warm liquid is spraying me. I'm never going to be the same again," she groans. "The worst part is, I'm getting used to the smell. I won't know if I still stink for days."

I force myself not to laugh. Her pout is adorable. I want to ask how that is even possible, but I force my mind to focus on what's important instead: getting her out of here and cleaned up so she won't be embarrassed any further.

"Come on. I have an outside shower I've rigged up. I'll help you." The offer is out of my mouth before I realize what I'm doing. I could kick myself. I can't have her over.

I suppose if this is how I'm punished for the choices I make in life, I shouldn't complain.

"You don't need to do that," she argues, taking a step to push her cart.

I step toward her, even though the smell has my eyes tearing, and I take charge. I move her cart to the cashier.

"I've never been so embarrassed in my life," she mumbles, watching everyone staring at us.

Her comment has me smiling, but then I realize it's not because she's embarrassed but it's because this is the one way I can help her.

"I got this. Wait outside so you don't have to go through explaining what happened to everyone."

"I'm sure everyone knows by now." She sighs. "Thank you, Max." She walks out of the store, looking defeated.

"Douche, good choice, sir." A young male rings up the items. He says it with a straight face. I have to give him some credit; I don't think I could have said the same thing with a straight face.

"It gets the rectum nice and clean," I reply, looking as serious as the kid. He stops what he's doing and stares at me for a moment. I can't keep myself from laughing though, and he does the same. "It's to help with skunk smell."

He nods, but his face shows his mind is going somewhere dirty, like a smelly vagina or something. Who knows how kids think these days?

"An actual skunk. Get your head out of the gutter." I roll my eyes playfully. The act forces my attention to Sienna outside. This girl doesn't have a lucky bone in her, it seems.

The items are loaded into a large brown paper bag and I meet her outside. She tries to take the bag from my arms but I refuse to allow her. That smell is awful. I want to ask if she can still smell it, but I don't want to come off as insensitive.

"I don't think we have to worry about a bobcat sneaking up on us," she tries to joke.

I don't respond. Really, what is there to say? We walk back to our places in silence. I like that she doesn't try to cover it with small talk.

"Would you mind going into my house to get me clothes? I don't want my stench to linger in there." Her cheeks grow rosy as she asks.

"Sure." I hand the bag off to her and she drops her keys in my hand. Walking in, her suitcase is open on the floor, looking like she's living out of it. That's new. It wasn't like that the other day.

I grab her shorts and a shirt, purposely omitting any underwear. There's a part of me that wants to walk right back outside and demand she wear one of my shirts. The thought hits hard. I can't have thoughts like that now. She has to be a job. I'd almost forgotten.

Shit. I rub my hand down my face, and for the first time ever, my eyes feel tired, overwhelmed.

I march out of her house and close the door with more force than necessary. I would love to wield a knife in my hand, but since I can't do that, I wish I could crack a textbook open. My thoughts are too jumbled, and I can't stand that. Too many thoughts are never a good thing.

"All good?" I glance up and see Sienna staring at me.

My lips try to lift into a believable smile. "Of course."

We make the short trek to my house, and I place her clothes on my back porch as I turn on the propane to heat the water for the outside shower.

"I used it this morning, so it shouldn't take longer than a few minutes."

I have a white board already sitting outside and I begin to tackle the problem I left on it. Without thinking, I pick up my favorite knife, twisting the sharp edge on the wood, my one finger staying on the handle as I allow myself to unjumble my thoughts by working on the whiteboard. Immediately, my shoulders relax, my brain is able to focus on one thing and I'm able to breathe easier.

It takes me a few minutes to solve, and when I glance up, Sienna is smiling at me. "What are you working on?" she asks.

I allow the knife to fall to the wood and slip it in the corner. "It's a physics question that I haven't been able to solve for the last day."

"You look like you enjoy studying."

I consider what she says. "I seem to have a hobby of collecting honoree degrees. I'm currently working on a computer science one."

"How many do you have?"

"This will be my fourth one. One of my teachers growing up told me that I had no self discipline and that's why I'd never graduate. He just didn't know that I had completed all the courses already, and just went to school for the fun of it. That was when my father allowed it."

I always imagined that when I told someone this, I would see pity or shock on their face. Instead, I watch as her face grows understanding, and yet my father's voice becomes louder.

You're worthless. You think this girl wants anything more than your help? You're crazy. I can't believe I wasted a sperm on you. You can't even pass class when you attend. At least you can be useful on the streets. I shove my father's voice away. Sometimes it's so loud I have to cover my ears.

I clear my throat, trying to concentrate through my inner demon. "What do you do, Sienna?"

She nibbles on her full bottom lip and my eyes linger there for a second. The darkness in me wants to bite her lip and have a taste. "I used to bookkeep for my family, and bartend. I've been making drinks since I was ten years old. I used to study how to bottle flip and make drinks, like you do with those numbers."

I already know she's twenty-three and her dad used to bring her everywhere until she sprouted tits. Instead of thinking how I would love to bite down on her pouty lips, I should be thinking that she's far too young for me. Still so innocent in the mileage of years. I'm fifteen years older than her and have seen my share of evil. Her father included.

Come to think of it, he's the reason I fell in obsession with her. I was planning on killing him, but became side tracked when I saw her. It's ironic that now they want me to kill her. I've never had to deal with a dilemma like this one before.

"A bartender, huh? Now, there's a talent I don't have. I bet you never had a slow day in your life once you stepped behind the counter." I lean into the movie quote from *Cocktail,* but she's probably too young to understand it. "I see America drinking the fabulous cocktails I make. Americans getting stinky on something I stir or shake. The sex on the beach."

"The schnapps made from peach, the velvet hammer, the Alabama slammer," she adds, right in line with the quote. "I love that movie. I used to want to bartend in some big fancy club, instead of the local watering hole."

I stand, otherwise I might act on the temptation of touching her. Checking the water, I find it's warm enough. I don't know how having her naked a few feet away from me is going to help any.

"Shower is ready. Hop on in while I get you a towel." Purposely, I "accidentally" knock over the cup of coffee I left from the morning and it runs over her shirt. "Shoot, I'm sorry. I'll grab you a shirt of mine you can wear."

I'm going to Hell. I guess nothing has changed. I smirk to myself, taking my time getting her a towel—a small one—and one of my shirts.

I step out to the sound of water spraying down. A light hum whispers past the water sound. I drape the items over the top of the walls caging her in. "Here you are."

I don't know why I torture myself this way. All I can imagine is her naked now.

Chapter 9: Max

♥

IT SHOULD BE ILLEGAL for someone to look as cute and beautiful as Sienna does in her hiking gear, or lack thereof. I glance down at her flip-flops and painted toenails. Her smooth skin glistens in the sun till her jean shorts cup her perfect, round ass. Each time she takes a step, it bounces and my hand wants to stretch out and cup hold of it. Would it be wrong if I fucked her, *then* did the murdering?

The one moral code I have is killing women, it just sits wrong with me.

She blushes and her hand brushes down her hair. "Do I have a bug on me?"

I chuckle. "Nope. I was just enjoying your hiking attire."

She raises a brow, looking me up and down. I have my spiked hiking boots laced up, jeans, and a large hiking backpack with plenty of water, rope, tape, and anything else I might need.

"I forgot, you're a nerd at heart," she teases me, pushing at my arm.

I bring out my bug spray and layer her with its mist. "I have you covered. You can thank me later." I wink.

"I've never been hiking before. Should I run back and change? I'm under prepared compared to you." Her self-consciousness radiates through her. The way she looks at me for guidance has my cock stirring. It's been a long time since I've felt anything. It's almost too bad I don't have time to play with Sienna before I have to end her.

"As you can tell, I'm more than prepared. I got ya."

I point in the direction of the trail. I've spent the last week building a few of my own paths back here.

The sky is blue, the birds welcoming us with their songs. Sienna keeps glancing at me from under her lashes, as if she's trying to steal looks in my direction.

"Are you hating it already?" I ask, and she stops taking a drink of her water. She's halfway done with the bottle and we've only walked for ten minutes. I underestimated how long this would take us.

"You seem in your element. I don't think I've seen you smile this much since I've met you."

I chuckle at her assessment. My veins are humming with the events to come. She would be running far away if she knew the real reason why I'm so happy today. I can't help it. Killing is in my blood. Not even the fact that it will be her dampens my good mood.

I begin to whistle and take the lead once again. She's way more talkative today than ever before.

"People do this to relax, right?" I look back, her brow is peppered with a light coating of sweat.

"I think that's the goal, or for fitness."

"Have I mentioned that I hate running or working out?" Her feet rush to stay caught up to mine.

I stop to look at her and she's able to catch up once again. "Then why did you agree to the hike?"

She stops, reaching to get a new bottle, but I beat her to it and bring out a white Powerade—it's one of her favorites—and open it for her.

"I love these!" she gushes, quenching her thirst by drinking a quarter of the bottle. I wonder how she will be about peeing in the bush. I have a feeling a girl like her might squirm at the idea.

She shrugs, answering my previous question. "You looked very excited about the idea, and I'd never done it before. Why did you move to Oakport Beach?" Her lashes flutter naturally, and the light is hitting her face to highlight how beautiful she is.

"Why did you?" I counter, not wanting to talk about myself. My mind is starting to wander once again. I push all thoughts out except for the task at hand.

"I needed to get away from family drama." I'm impressed how close to the truth that is.

"Family drama has a way of biting you in the ass when you least expect it," I reply. "But you guys must have made up. I saw your suitcase by the door. You leaving?"

She bites down on her lower lip, drawing my eyes to her mouth. She looks sheepish before she answers, but I already know. I know everything about her. "Yeah, it's time for a change of scenery. This town is too small for my liking. It's time to find a new place that I can hopefully call home."

Her leaving works perfect to the story line that will play out. By next month, no one will remember her ever having been in this town.

Sienna

I QUICKLY SWALLOW A quarter of my electrolyte drink in one gulp and a wheeze is released from my throat as I forego oxygen. I'm sweaty everywhere and can feel it trickle between my breasts.

Max, on the other hand, hasn't broken a sweat. He looks as handsome as ever. For once in my life, I've attracted a handsome, smart, regular man. It's really too bad I have to leave town. I can't chance the motorcycle club finding me. I would love to see where Max and I could have gone.

It's the only reason I said yes to a hike. Max walks up to me and takes a bandana from his pocket, wiping at my forehead before his hands cup my face. He stares into my eyes like he's trying to memorize whatever he sees.

"It's really too bad this will be the last time we see each other." His words have my heart speeding up, while igniting a flurry of butterflies in my stomach.

My head tilts up, gazing into his eyes. It takes all of my stubbornness to not cave and say fuck it to not leaving Oakport Beach. The town really would be a great place to put roots down in. I breathe him in. Maybe I could get into this hiking thing if we stuck around each other. Never in my mind would I have thought this if I had never met Max.

"I'm a firm believer of fate. If we're meant to see each other again, it will happen." I step away, worried he'll suck me in and I'll never go through with my plan.

Max clears his throat, taking a step back as well. He gives me this shy, handsome look that sends a flutter down my spine.

"To fate it is then," he replies in a tone like he's in on some private joke.

We continue walking through the thick forest, visibility is less than an arm's length into the brush lining the small pathway. "This so-called view better be worth it," I joke behind him.

"It will get your heart racing." He smirks, turning back.

"Do you have siblings?" I ask, always wanting to know more about him, but he's quiet and doesn't divulge much about himself. It's like pulling strings to get anything out of him.

"I have an older brother, who has a wife, and two younger brothers."

"How much younger?"

He looks back at me. "About a decade."

I had figured Max was older than me, but I still can't pinpoint his age. Looks like I'm going to have to be more specific. "How old are you?"

He lifts one brow and looks to be debating about answering. He turns around, continuing on our hike. Just when I think he isn't going to answer, he says, "I'm almost forty."

He looks good for his age. I study his ass and his muscular legs with appreciation.

"Anything else you want to know? We're almost there."

My lips purse and twist as I consider what else I want to know. "Where did you grow up?"

He snorts. "A pig farm, it was awful."

"Is that why you like the outdoors?"

He ignores my question. "We're here," he announces. I look around us, and there's no view. In the distance, there could be a cave of some sort. Maybe? Bush is all around us, looking like the rest of the forest we trampled through.

"Is this the turning back point? I thought...I don't know what I thought," I say, disappointed in the view while turning in a full circle, confused as to why we would come here.

When I face Max, he has a gun pointed at me. My heart leaps into my throat and I stare, stunned. It's like my brain can't comprehend what's happening. I look from the gun to him, multiple times, as I stay perfectly frozen.

"This isn't personal. If it makes you feel better, you were the highlight of the last few months of mine."

I've only met him. Slowly, like my brain is just starting to claw its way out of cobwebs to get a better view, I realize he's going to kill me. My heart hammers, a cold chill rakes over me as the atmosphere changes on a dime.

"Run." His voice has lowered, deepening into a harsh breath.

My muscles don't hesitate and I run into the bush, trying to get away. Twigs snap against me, scraping my skin as I go. The deeper I travel, the more my legs feel the lashing of the forest. I'm the only noise in the silence, and I keep expecting to hear the snap of a bullet, but it refuses to come. My chest tightens, my heartbeat erratic with each deep breath I'm forced to take. No steps crash behind me, but I refuse to look, too scared to see him on my heels.

Each breath I take is like tiny razors brushing down my throat with each deep gasp. My legs are on fire from the strain. I don't know if I can keep going. I don't even know if I'm going the right way. The only thing I know is that I've lost him.

I break back onto a trail, hunching over my legs, wheezing, hoping to get my breath under control. There's ringing in my ears and my stomach wants to unleash onto the ground.

"You're even more gorgeous scared." Max's deep voice has me squealing and trying to sprint off again, but his strong arm pulls me back, crushing me into his thick chest.

My heart jumps wildly and my mouth dries, but I refuse to go down without a fight. I thrust against him, my tears overflowing onto my cheeks. "Please, don't kill me," I beg, continuing to fight, but he's too strong. My attempts to free myself do nothing but trap me against his muscular body.

"Sorry, darling. This is what I do best. It's what my father trained me for."

I kick as hard as I can but he doesn't even flinch. How had I read him entirely wrong? I grew up with killers and bad men my whole life. I know the type. Panic grips my brain, his body warming the terror that has every hair standing on end.

I scream until my voice is hoarse and it crackles as I try to speak. "Please, let me go," I plead with a low voice. Tears stream down like a tsunami wave. "I'm not ready to die. I want to live and fall in love. I'll disappear, you'll never see me again. Do you need money? My dad can pay you." It all rushes out between hushed sobs.

He lets a manic laugh out of his throat. His whole body vibrates against mine as if I just said the funniest joke he's ever heard.

"Your father? It was his club who ordered the hit."

I stop struggling and go limp in his hold. "But why?" I already know. They think I killed my husband. "I didn't do what they think." Realization that I spent my last day on Earth hiking dawns on me. I wasted my last day.

"I know. I did." His hot breath fans across my ear and I jerk in surprise, replaying what I think he said. I must have heard wrong. I thrash in his hold, but my violent struggles seem to be unnoticed as he puts little effort into keeping me in place.

"I'm the loose end." Goosebumps pepper my skin. "If you let me go, no one will ever know you didn't kill me." I give it one more attempt to save my soul and try to kick him in the nuts and run. My body refuses to move in his tight grasp. "It would be like our private joke on them."

I wiggle some more, not ready for this to be the end. "Please, do me this one favor. I'll do anything you want. I will be in your debt forever." I know it's no use, but my self-preservation has kicked in.

"So, you want to owe me." His deep voice dances across my skin and my body stops moving.

"Yes, yes, I do!" Once again, my voice breaks at the end.

"For this to work, you have to go where I tell you. If they find you, I'm as good as dead like you'll be."

I can't believe my ears. It can't be this easy, it has to be a trick. His hold loosens and my feet slip down to find a solid footing on the ground. Every nerve in my body wants to run again, but if I do, he could change his mind. There's no way I can outrun him, but I could outsmart him, given enough space.

"I promise," I vow, still trying to catch my breath.

He's studying me, his eyes roaming from my eyes all the way to my feet, which are screaming for me to run. It takes all of my willpower to stay in the presence of a murderer.

"Here's a card." He opens his backpack and digs his hand around, searching. "You need to get a job here." He hands the small rectangle of thick paper over. *Throne of Sin* is emblazoned in gold lettering with a stripper pole on the right, with a silhouette.

I'm already judging the fact I've left one Hell hole for another, unfortunately, it's what I know best.

"Never thought of myself as a stripper." I scratch my head.

"Says the girl who was begging for her life," he says sharply, grabbing hold of my wrist as his other hand wraps around the back of my neck.

I cock a brow. "I didn't say I was complaining," I defend while standing tall in his hold, but I can't stop my lips from trembling.

"They need a bartender. Stripping is optional." Max winks while slowly looking me over with a new hunger in his eyes. He releases his hold on me and my body slouches back, exhausted from the events that just transpired.

We stare at each other and I'm left with no other option but to trust the man.

"It's like the job was made for me." I begin to walk past him, keeping my fake bravery up. "Come on, boy, let's go." His hand shoots out, grasping hold of my forearm, and forcefully brings me back into him. I hold my breath, scared of what will happen next.

"Hold on a second."

I didn't think my heart could beat faster than it was before, but here it is. My hand covers my erratic heartbeat, scared I might die from a heart attack instead of being murdered. No matter how hard I clench my muscles, they frantically vibrate in his hold.

Max's savage attention stays on me. Violence flares in his deep blue eyes. This is not the look of a good man. A destructive energy coils, wrapping us thickly. My ears ring from the extra blood, while he's looking relaxed, absent the murderous gaze in his eyes.

A small smile settles on his face and I think he might be enjoying this. I fear if I fight him, he'll change his mind and I'll be...gone. Forgotten. There's no one left to remember me. That's maybe the saddest part of this. No one will miss me.

"I'll drive you there, but you're on your own for the rest." He pauses, waiting for me to shake my head in understanding. "If you deviate from the plan, I'll kill you before they have the chance to."

My mouth is dry, making it impossible to swallow the small amount of saliva on my tongue. His eyes hold a cruel promise.

I place my hand on his bicep and look him in the eyes. The air thickens around us, sparking with energy. It's like nothing I've ever felt before. "You can trust me, I promise."

He lets me go, like I've burned him. He seems taller, broader now. He's not this man who hasn't grown into his legs yet, but an intimidating beast. Each of his strides are purposeful. He takes one, I take two, but he still manages to nudge my shoulder.

"Walk," he demands. I jump at the edginess of his rough voice and move. We stay silent, even when we return to my little cottage. The only thing heard over the birds is the sound of my heavy breathing as I grab my suitcase and get into his vehicle.

Chapter 10: Sienna

♥

*W*AKE UP, YOU HAVE *a shift to start.* I keep repeating the sentiment to myself, willing my heavy lids to open. Little by little, one eye, then the other flutters open. I quickly squeeze them shut against the glaring sun trying to laser my eyes out of my sockets. *Did dad fix the boarded-up window?*

I shoot straight up from the bed. It's all coming back to me. The gun. Max. A road trip? There should have been a road trip...

"Max?" I call, standing so fast my head whirls with a sudden dizziness. My feet are unsteady, each step wobbly, and I rest a hand on the wall as my world straightens itself.

Silence answers in return. There isn't even a ticking sound from a clock or electric hum of appliances in general.

I need to get out of here. I pat myself down. I'm still in the hiking gear I had on earlier.

Where am I? Taking in my surroundings, I cautiously step out of a tiny bedroom that is barely big enough for the single bed I was on. There's a table with a hot plate and a dingy couch that gives me the shivers. I'm on edge, waiting for Max to jump out of nowhere. *Why isn't he here?*

I glance out the window, the view giving no indication of where *here* is. I could be in Alaska for all I know. I hate the cold...

Please don't say I'm in Alaska.

My eyes search the small space. No Max. My pulse slows slightly, but I stay on edge. On top of the hot plate is the card for Throne of Sin. The gold lettering taunts me and an eerie shiver dances through my body. I take the card, my shaky fingers ripping it into a million little pieces, and I watch them scatter to the floor like big, soft, fluttering, snowflakes.

I'm out of here. I swiftly walk toward the door before a distant ring catches my attention. The sound has my feet marching toward it and into the bedroom. A phone rests on the pillow that was next to my head and I eye it like it holds the plague. My hand hovers over the device, unsure if I should pick it up, and retreats when the sound stops. No more than a second later, its angry sound begins again.

Nope, not happening. I run out the front door, but a strong arm catches me around the waist, my feet lift from the ground, and I scream at the top of my lungs. A hand wraps around my face, hauling me inside before I'm pushed against a wall.

A *tski*ng sound vibrates over my skin. "Already disobeying me, Sienna? This is not a good start." Max's hard features come into view.

I move my jaw, hoping to nip him, but the pressure is too great. "I'm going to uncover your mouth and you're going to have to be a good girl. But before I do, I'll let you in on a little secret." He leans down, his lips hovering over my ear. "I find you incredibly sexy when you scream." Finger by finger, his hand releases my face.

"I just woke up. I have no idea what you're talking about," I lie.

"You ripped up the card I left for you." A cold chill races over me, sending my skin into a canvas of pebbled bumps. I swallow, not responding. Max's short breaths fill the silence. "I'm your only chance of survival now. Everyone already thinks you're dead." His pointer finger brushes down the side of my face. "Don't look so scared."

Max takes a step back, watching each of my moves.

"Are you going back on your word?" His lethal tone booms through the room.

I straighten to my full height. "I don't need reminders."

"Be a good girl, and go to Throne of Sin. I left a change of clothes in the closet."

Max gives me a wink, handing me a single key that I assume is for this place. I have no intention of coming back here once I leave, the joke will be on him.

"Oh, and Sienna, if you don't come back, that friend of yours...what's her name again? Ginevra? I'll make sure she disappears. It would be such a shame, having her family lose her when they have already dealt with so much with her father's passing…" He threatens my one and only friend before striding out through the door.

Doing a quick map search, I find that the club is just a few blocks from here. I intentionally leave the phone behind, wanting to make a quick escape, but there's a darkness that follows me. I see no one, but I know he is there watching. It's that same feeling I've had for over a month.

The large Throne of Sin neon sign blinks at me. I can't believe I'm being bullied into this, but here goes. I walk in with a smile on my face, hoping to blend in, but all eyes fall on me. I stick out, and the girls eye me as I walk further in. The women look like the regular groupies from the motorcycle club who are all hoping to become an old lady. They have makeup plastered to their faces and wear clothes one size too small on their already-skeletal bodies. I glance down at myself. I have a healthy dose of cushion and look nothing like these girls. It's obvious I already don't fit in.

I walk right back outside to find Max standing on the opposite sidewalk. He lifts his hand and places a cigarette into his mouth and lights it with a lighter. Our eyes lock on to each other, the connection unwavering as we stare. I wouldn't be able to pull away if I wanted to, it's like two ends of a magnet and they're being forced together no matter what you want as an outcome.

He takes a drag before he points back to the entrance. My feet hesitate to leave, because I still can't look away. It's a sin for Max to look so gorgeous when I know he's not a good man. It's deceiving and misleading, providing me with a horrible experience.

He turns his back, our connection severing immediately, and I turn to go back into the building.

"Change your mind?" The bouncer chuckles.

I give him a tight smile while squaring my shoulders. I go to the counter, watching the bartender on shift. He's preppier than the clientele. Clean cut, suit, and expensive watch. Despite my best efforts, my nervousness rolls through me. I've never worked for anyone but my father. "I'm looking for Dante Mancini."

The bartender turns. "Who wants to know?"

"I heard he needs another bartender, and I have experience. Is he in? I don't have time to sit around. If he's not, I'll be on my way." I wince at my straightforward tone, knowing it must be coming off bitchy. I can't help it, my nerves are getting the best of me. I pick at the nail bed on my thumb as I wait for an answer.

The man raises his hand to shake mine, not looking put off by my attitude. "It's only fair I know your name, if you know mine."

My jaw drops, not expecting him to be the owner. He looks much too young. He can't be older than me. Well, now I'm definitely not getting the job with that first impression.

"Sienna," I introduce.

"You have a last name, darlin'?"

"Not one that anyone needs to know."

He nods his head like he understands. "That's the beauty here. You can be anyone you want. By all means, come behind and show me what you've got."

I walk around, eyeing all the liquors, the tall wall of bottles holding more options than I'm used to. Within a minute, I'm wowing him with my moves and my fancy cocktails. It takes no effort to make five drinks, flip bottles, and do a flirty turn, before I'm done and looking at him expectantly.

Instead of him looking impressed, he's eyeing me like I'm crazy. "Listen, New York. Here it's rum and Cokes, gin and tonics, or beer. Those fancy liquors are for tourists who get lost and find themselves here." My chest deflates. "Can you count as well as you bottle flip?"

"Yes, Sir."

"Good, you start now. If you survive the rush, you're hired on."

Chapter 11: Max

♥

S IENNA IS FUCKING GORGEOUS. The sight of her has my pulse racing, and the way she holds my stare makes my cock hard. I'm second guessing if I should have forced her into my brother's strip club. The only reason I keep with my original decision is that I know Dante would rather watch his girls than touch them, and he's loyal to a fault. No one touches his girls. She will be safe there. Possibly a little too safe, even from me, if she keeps this job.

When I'm certain she's staying at Throne of Sin for the next few hours, I jump onto my motorcycle and head towards my other brother Romeo's place. He's the Don of our family.

Walking into the butcher shop, the smell brings back memories of the days he and I lived on a pig farm. Back in a time when we were banished after our father's death. As much as I hate emotional attachments, the smell of this place brings warmth and comfort to me.

I find my brother in the back office. "What's up, fucker?"

He looks up, a smile gracing his lips as he stands, coming to give me a welcoming hug.

"I knew that job would get you out of that whole moping around needing a vacation thing." He pats my back, stepping back to assess me. My brother and I have never kept secrets from each other, until now. We've had to claw our way to where we are after our father fucked everything up and got himself killed. Remembering everything we've gone through together has guilt squeezing my heart, until I push it out.

"We're never working for them again. Involving us in that motorcycle club's business is not a good look," I tell him, angry over the predicament it has placed me in.

He levels me with a look, not used to me showing any emotion. "I figured we owed them since you killed and scattered a lot of them around the country."

"I told you they weren't all mine. Plus, the ones who were, deserved it."

The letters have continued to arrive for me, and they are coming closer together. It's frightening how much this crazy knows. It has me more on edge than I'd like to admit. Not that anyone knows about it.

Romeo sighs. "They always do."

I WALK INTO SIENNA'S micro apartment like I own it. She may have been a little shocked when she woke up, but I think she'll like it here. I look around while turning in a circle. Yeah, this place has a good vibe. She's still at Throne of Sin, and I want to make her first night special when she returns. I have a bottle of red wine and a container of Chinese takeout. I open the wine, allowing it to breathe before setting two glasses down beside it. My steps have an extra bounce as I go sit on the couch to wait for her.

I imagine all of her facial expressions and can't wait to see which one I'll get when she sees me. My foot vibrates with anticipation of her arrival.

I consider waiting on her small balcony, but I want to see her reaction up close.

The door opens and she doesn't bother turning on the lights. Her attention focuses on her bedroom light that she shut off this morning. My fingers curl into my thigh, refusing to stand and ruin my surprise. I love the way her pouty lips twist together in confusion. Her brows furrow when her gorgeous greens dart to the items I placed on her table.

I already know I should have stayed away, but I can't help myself. If I plan to continue stalking her, I should do it at a distance like every other one of my prey. I scratch at my chin. The problem is, she's nothing like I've ever experienced before.

My movements catch her attention, and she jumps, screaming when she finally spots me. Her hand flies to her chest, her breasts heaving up and down with each panicked breath.

"How was the first day?" I ask, standing. She takes a few steps away from the table as I pick up the wine and pour us a glass each.

"What the fuck, Max?" Her tone is harsh and she refuses to accept the glass of wine from me.

"Take the glass, Sienna," I demand, keeping the glass raised. I will not accept disobedience.

Her eyes narrow into a beautiful glare. My hand wants to reach out to feel her pulse jumping, but the urge to do her harm is nowhere. It's the strangest feeling.

"I can force you to drink it, or we can have an adult conversation."

She laughs at my comment, but takes the wine. "Thank you," I praise, bringing the wine to my lips. It hovers there until she does the same. A grin replaces my flat lips.

"Why do I have no memory of being brought here?" she asks, placing a hand on her hip.

I pull out a chair, silently asking her to sit. "You'll be more understanding once you have a belly full of food."

She huffs, stepping toward the chair. I pull mine out but refuse to sit before her. My right eyebrow cocks, waiting. I love that she is trying to defy me, but in the end, we both know she will be a good girl and do as she's told.

Sienna falls into her seat, the chair tipping backward slightly before it thuds back down. I try to keep my expression neutral even though a smirk is begging my lips to turn upward. I love that she obeys even when she doesn't want to.

Her arms are crossed over her chest and her frown refuses to smooth out. Her stubbornness is cute as Hell. No one challenges me like she can. Her body strums with a need to defy me, and I want to tell her this is helping the foreplay between us, but I don't think she'd get the same enjoyment out of it that I do. Her taut muscles refuse to move, causing me to chuckle as I dish our dinner out.

I bring my chair next to hers and our knees bump into each other. Her back straightens and her body goes even more rigid. Being this close has her perfume wrapping around me at every angle. She never had a chance against me, but I never expected us to be bonding over a shared dinner. I've been holding on to the notion that I had to stay away from her, but why? I remove her utensils, giving her time to protest, but her fuckable lips stay sealed. I spear a piece of sweet and sour pork with my fork, bringing it to her lips. She sucks in a ghastly breath, shaking her head.

"I thought we wanted to be adults here..." I state, pressing the meat to her nude-colored lips.

"You're fucking psycho—"

I jab the piece of food into her mouth before she can finish the sentence.

"I've been called much worse, but I have to admit, it does sound much more beautiful coming from your mouth." I spear some noodles and twirl them around the fork before lifting. Her fingers indicate she's still chewing without saying a word. I watch in fascination when she swallows with a bob. My imagination goes wild from the action and my cock hardens. It's like I'm a teen boy who just figured out how his dick works. In fact, I don't remember the last time a woman made my dick do anything. I thought I'd lost that part of myself. Killing has been my lover for the last few years.

Once again, she refuses by shaking her head. I narrow my eyes and she opens her mouth to argue, "I can fucking—"

I slip the food in with a chuckle, enjoying myself.

Her hand reaches out, grasping mine. A current zaps through me, and she must feel it too. Her hand loosens before she tries to grab the utensil from me. "I can do it myself."

I'm not giving this up. "Next time, when I ask you to eat, do it and I won't have to help you. You're stuck with me feeding you now. The faster we eat, the faster we can enjoy our wine and talk."

Surprisingly, she opens her mouth, waiting for her next mouthful. I feed her in silence. It's not awkward, but rather enjoyable, even though her face isn't portraying how I'm feeling. This is her favorite type of takeout, I would think she'd at least comment on the fact. She used to order this type of stuff three times a week.

When her plate is empty, I begin on mine. I've never had a meal taste so delicious. It has to be the company. She drinks her wine and I pour her a second glass as I'm finishing up.

"Now, you must be feeling better." I stand, clearing the table, before sitting on the couch. My hand pats the seat next to me. Her face transforms and a fake mask slips on.

She walks over, drink in hand, and lays down, placing her feet on me. Taking a sip of my wine, I set it on the coffee table and begin to rub at her feet. What is she playing at? Whatever game she thinks she's playing, I can play too.

"The travel across different states was going to be long and boring. I slipped you something to make you more comfortable." I answer her original question.

"Where are we?"

"We're back in Texas, under your father's nose. He'll never look for you here, and I can assure your safety this way."

"We need boundaries, Max."

Boundaries...

Not, *get the hell away from me*. I can work with this.

"We're not going to start lying to each other. This is who we are. No boundaries are needed, not that I'd heed whatever you want to place forward," I respond, and she slips her foot from my hand, her angry face back in full force.

"Max," she growls, her forehead ruffling. "No more drugging me." She stands, pointing. "I mean it. I don't like not being in control." She says it with such a sad face, who am I to refuse her request?

"Fine. No more drugging," I concede.

"You need to knock like a regular person."

I hold up my hand. "Neither of us are normal people. You got one request. That's enough for now." I stand, placing my wine on the counter.

"Have a good night, Sienna." I leave, letting myself out. My body pauses just before I shut the door. "Don't forget to lock the door." The door is almost closed when I add, "And Sienna, don't be getting any crazy thoughts. If you run, it will either be me or your family killing you."

R OMEO SENT ME OUT of town over a week ago and my anxiety is through the roof. I've read at least two thick textbooks while dealing with a rat who became too chummy with a fucking undercover cop, but in doing so I had to leave Sienna unattended.

It feels like I have spiders running through my veins. Even now, seeing Sienna from across the street, the squirming feeling doesn't disappear. I step closer, needing to be near her. Her ass sways with each confident step she takes. She's wearing a shorter shirt that shows off a sliver of gorgeous skin.

I'm entranced by her and my feet continue to follow, my eyes never straying. I give her a few minutes to enter Throne of Sin before I walk in, trying to stay in the shadows. I don't need my brothers asking me questions.

My mouth dries when I watch Sienna give my brother a hug. Instantly, the image of me stabbing him pushes its way into my mind's eye. The only thing saving him is the way he tenses and shoves her away. She shrugs it off, continuing with her job.

I know she's safe here, but seeing that hug has me questioning if I should stay here for the rest of the night. My fingers tap against each other as I watch Dante go into his office before I head toward her place to set up the desperately needed cameras. With each step, my agitation decreases and I begin to whistle as my excitement builds, knowing I'm going to be in Sienna's personal space. Twirling her keys around my finger, I unlock her door without care. My feet halt, my torso leaning over my feet as I stare at what looks like a six-foot bear that's growling. His teeth are pointed and drool hangs over his weapon of a mouth.

Immediately, I close the door and relock it. This is a small little bump in the road, but nothing I can't fix.

I'm back within a half hour with a McDonald's ice cream cone in hand. The teeth become smaller and I'm able to slip inside and close the door, but he doesn't retreat. I move my hand closer to the brute of a dog and allow him to smell what I have. I'm risking my hand, but it will be worth it to have this animal on my side.

He snaps his teeth and I marginally get to keep my fingers, but I watch his big black nose twist and move, smelling the gift I've brought. Once again, I bring the vanilla cone up and his tongue cautiously dips out. It allows me to step closer and bring my hand out for him to smell. Another lick of the sweet dessert and I'm able to pat his head.

"What's your name, fella?" I ask, holding the now-dripping ice cream while the dog continues with his leisurely licks. "I'll just call you Brute until Sienna tells me otherwise. You want to help me install some cameras?"

Chapter 12: Sienna

"SHELBY WON'T COME OUT from the back." I turn my head seeing one of Dante's girls staring at me expectantly. Boss man is gone and these girls keep looking at me like I'm their leader.

"Watch the bar," I instruct while going into the changing rooms.

Shelby is standing there shaking like a leaf. "First time on stage?" I ask.

She shakes her head. "It's Denver, my old dealer, and..." She clears her throat, tilting her head like I should know the rest of it. "He can't see me here. I'm finally free of him. I can't go back."

Now, this is something I can understand. I lift a finger and walk out.

It takes me less than three seconds to get the bouncers' attention and they're moving to remove this asshole before I finish my last breath.

I go back into the changing room. "Problem is gone. Everyone's been notified that he's not to ever step foot in here again. We good now?" I can hear the crowd getting rowdy, expecting a girl to be dancing on stage and becoming bored with no entertainment.

The building is over capacity with a raw edge of energy thriving between the walls. I can't help but to continually glance at the entrance, expecting to see someone from my world. It's been a while since I've seen or heard from Max, and it's unnerving. People in this lifestyle don't live very long, maybe he's met his maker. I'm not sure what to think of that. Am I happy or sad?

By the time the lights turn on at the end of the night, my feet are throbbing, but I'm not close to being tired. Dante walks in looking like he just woke up and showered in his perfectly fitted suit. This guy looks flawless all the time. It has to be exhausting.

"Is this your version of fashionably late?" I holler while I weigh the bottles from behind.

The air in the room changes and the low chatter dies down immediately. Maybe this guy doesn't know how to joke? He strides toward me with his long legs and stops to narrow his eyes. I can't tell if it's a glare or a general assessment.

"What did you say to me?"

Oh, fuck me, another one with an ego. Problem is, I'm used to not being able to keep my mouth shut. I know the consequences, I'm just unworried about it. Some call it stupid, but I refuse to regard myself in that way.

"Not in the joking mood tonight, Boss Man?" I lean my hip against the bar. "When was the last time you got laid?"

His face before was an assessment, now it's a glare. I place my hand over his, trying to smooth the water, and he jumps back like I've burned him. He has to have an anti-touching thing going on. This man needs to be socialized. He owns a strip club, for goodness sakes, and that's the honest part of the business.

"Here's the thing, we need to make a few changes." I grab another bottle, placing it on the scale.

Dante's eyes bulge out like he's a cartoon, but he remains silent. "This crowd wants something that no one else offers. You should place a viewing area in one of the rooms. Then you can charge for watching and people will pay more to be in the room with the viewing opportunities. You'd make a killing." *And maybe this will put a smile on your face.*

I continue on rambling about the night, but out of the corner of my eye I watch his lips purse back and forth as he thinks about my suggestion.

I don't even think he's paying me any more attention when he says, "I heard about Shelby tonight, thanks for taking care of that. I've ensured he won't be a problem here again." He taps his fist on the counter three times. "It looks like you can handle yourself pretty well. I need help with scheduling, and if this all continues to work out, if you need more hours, I have some bookkeeping you can do." My ears perk up with the extra hours. More hours equal the faster I can get out of here and be on my way. "But don't ever tell me how to run my club again."

My smile grows as he walks away. He loved my suggestion, I can tell. I giggle before schooling my expression and keep my head down while continuing my task.

DANTE HAS WALKED ME home each night for the last two weeks. In that short amount of time, he's become closer to me than any of my family. I can't help but think of him like a brother. He has this protectiveness that spreads to all the girls in his club. I now understand why Max sent me to work here. No one touches anything of Dante's.

Max. I hate that I'm thinking about him again. The fucker is dead, has to be, because a stalker doesn't just up and leave.

"What has you so preoccupied tonight?" Dante questions in the dark of the night.

"Huh?" His voice pulls me out of my thoughts. "Sorry, just thinking about the money you'll make off my fantastic suggestion." I smirk, bumping him with my shoulder as we walk.

"I don't know what the fuck you're talking about."

"No? You have no idea about that two-way mirror being placed into one of the walls of the back rooms?" It took him a week before the construction crew started to come in during the day when we weren't open.

"Fuck off." He laughs, bumping me back.

The area has a few lamp posts that highlight the sidewalk, but over half are burned out and need replacing. I feel for my hidden knife sheathed at my waist, as a protective comfort. Remembering that I stole the knife from Max has my lips curling up.

Like every other night, Dante stays outside my building until he sees a light go on in my place. The light inside the hall flickers annoyingly as I make it up the steps to my apartment. I shoulder open the door with the extra pressure I typically need, expecting my dog to be sleeping at the bottom of it. He lays at the base of the doorway each time I leave and doesn't move until I return.

I fly into my home, no dog blocking the access. A light by the window flickers on from my motion before I have the chance to turn on the light at the entrance. My heart leaps into my throat, knowing that Dante thinks I'm inside. *Where the fuck is my dog?* The light quickly turns off, leaving me back in the dark.

I hesitate, trying to turn on my lights, but the bulb above the door is burned out. "Griffin?" I whisper, hoping to hear the clunky sound of my dog getting up.

Nothing.

I take my knife out, keeping it in front of me as I move deeper in, but keeping the door open. The adrenaline has every muscle shaking, and the knife vibrates back and forth in hand.

I wait for my eyes to adjust to the dark. It takes a second before I see Griffin lying on the couch, fast asleep. *Please let him be sleeping.* I love this dog too much to have anything happen to him, and I'm not even a dog person. I place my hand on him, *warm*. My eyes close with relief until I see a figure moving as they try to sit up.

A piercing scream leaves my mouth as I jab with my knife.

"Mother fucker," a deep voice curses and I push the knife deeper. Griffin is no help and lets the man up from under him. In fact, his tail wags, unaware of the stranger who shouldn't be in my house.

"Sienna, it's me." A rough hand grabs mine, twisting it until I have to let go of the knife. It doesn't clatter to the ground and I watch as Max has to pull it out of his bicep. Blood seeps out, his hand pressing over it.

I try to see his face but it's too dark.

"What the hell are you doing in here? I thought you were dead." I march to the front door, slamming it before twisting the dead bolt and flicking the lights on by the couch.

He chuckles, walking around me to grab a cloth, which he places on his wound. "Not even death itself can keep me away from you." It sounds like he's trying to flirt with me.

"My dog should have killed you." I place my hands on my hips.

"Naw, we became friends weeks ago, when I shared an ice cream with him."

"Weeks ago?"

He pats Griffin on the head, their faces turning toward each other, and Griffin nuzzles into his leg.

"Yea, Brute and I are good friends now. We both like to watch you sleep at night."

A very unladylike growl escapes my lips. "You have to stop doing this." I pinch the bridge of my nose. "And his name is Griffin." I almost stomp my foot with the way Max is driving me crazy.

"Nope, he answers to Brute, I'm keeping it. But let's circle back to you being worried about me and thinking I was dead." He's smiling at me and I want to stab him again. Why does he get to look all cocky and handsome while I'm just coming off a long shift?

Max slides out a chair and I know it's pointless to stand while my feet are throbbing. I drop down, placing my head into my hands. My eyes hurt and I need sleep.

"Max, go home. I'm exhausted."

"Home is where the heart is," he comments, his voice coming closer to me. Pressure is felt on my shoulders and I jump at the sudden unexpected touch.

My head lifts and he steps away to lean against a wall, looking casual and at ease. "You tried to kill me less than a month ago." Why is he making me say this out loud? "We are not friends, Max."

His hand brushes over his chin. "Are you going to hold that against me forever?" He lets out a chuckle and I stand, going into my room.

I don't bother closing the door, knowing it won't bar him, and keep my back to the bedroom entrance. I change out of my shirt and slip into a nightgown before shimmying out of my shorts.

"Look at us bickering like an old married couple," he says from behind.

Max is completely clueless. "Not a couple, Max. Just a girl with her stalker."

Fuck me, now I'm sounding like him.

I slip under my covers. "Lock the door on your way out, and turn off my light please." The room grows dark instantly and my heavy eyes are no match for the darkness. I fall asleep within seconds, knowing I'm safe with Max here.

Chapter 13: Sienna

♥

I'VE BECOME USED TO Max's presence everywhere. I see him as I walk to work, in the far distance, just watching. When I don't see him, my body naturally tenses, always looking for trouble.

Even tonight, he's in the dark shadows of the ballroom, just watching, brooding. It sends an inexplicable shiver down my spine.

"You cold?" Dante asks, taking a break from talking to another man. I could tell him right now and Max would be history. *I can take care of myself.* Dante has been so kind and welcoming to me, there's no point in dragging him into my mess. It wouldn't be fair.

"No, just a shiver." I stand, wanting to give myself some space, and I know Dante needs to talk business without me by his side.

My entire focus is on the way my skin warms with Max's eyes on me. It's the most ridiculous thing ever. I'm no better than the club girls back home. Straightening my spine, I work the room, keeping my attention on everyone I'm talking to. There's no one I don't talk to, because I know that everything in life is about *who* you know, not *what* you know.

My skin begins to chill and I already know Max has left. I don't need to look in the shadows to be sure.

"You must be the prettiest girl here," a man named Jameson compliments, kissing my hand. I already know his type and slip my fingers from his hold. He's eyeing me like he knows who I am, and it makes me uneasy.

My muscles strain, but I keep my smile on my face. "Excuse me, my date, Dante, is waiting."

He looks behind me, and it's obvious Dante isn't missing me. "Ah, yes, he and I go way back. Enjoy your night."

I leave, walking straight to the bathroom. Each breath is difficult to take as I hold on to the counter and stare at myself in the mirror. No one knows who I am. Everything is fine.

My hands clumsily turn on the tap and splash water over my face. The need for the sanctuary of my small apartment calls to me for the first time since I've moved in a few months ago.

"You must be the most dangerous woman here." The echo of a deadbolt sounds around me. I splash more water on my face, cleaning the mascara that has chosen to run, while ignoring Max. I can feel the energy vibrate off him as I pretend he's not there. It eats at him, driving him crazy. I shouldn't poke the bear but it helps to remind me that I'm here.

"If you let another man touch you, I'll kill each and every one, including Dante."

I've never dealt well with threats from anyone before. It has my tongue lashing out before I can think. "You would kill the man who you left me to for safekeeping when you can't do your own job?"

"Can you handle another death on your conscience?" he counters with a predatory gleam in his eyes.

"Another? When was the first one?"

"When they threw you in the swamp and laughed."

I freeze, slowly turning toward him. "Excuse me?" I ask shakily.

"You heard me. Everyone that night who took advantage and laughed at you is gone. You're welcome." His voice is hard with an edge. Looking into his eyes, his face is set like stone, serious, and absent any signs of a joke.

"Dante is a good man," I choke out, not wanting him to be harmed.

Max steps closer to me, grasping my chin with his fingers. "I know. He's my brother, but when it comes to you, no one gets any leniency. I have no problem killing him and sleeping like a baby afterwards."

"You would kill your own brother?" I say in disbelief, not realizing the family connection.

He's staring me in the eyes, his grip strong. "I would kill anyone for you."

"You're fucking crazy." I swat at his hands and they release my chin. He's already killed for me. I turn away from him, grasping the counter once again.

"Crazy for you, Sienna. Only you. The sooner you come to terms with this the better."

I stare at him through the mirror, his face distorting into something tender and warm. Quick as a flash, his mood can change instantly.

"Let me take you home. I know you don't want to be here any longer." I wish I could argue, but the truth is I want to leave.

"Griffin needs a walk still. I didn't get a chance to do it earlier."

"We'll walk Brute together." I ignore the fact he's renamed my dog and follow his lead once he places his hand on my lower back.

I get no message from Dante wondering where I went. When I double-check my phone, Max's smirk grows as if he knows what I'm checking, but good for him he doesn't comment.

Stepping out of his car, he leaves it in a no-parking zone. Once again, I zip my lips. If he wants his car towed, it's his own problem.

Max makes himself at home gathering Griffin's stuff. The big lug is even happier to see him than me. "Oh, stop pouting." He nudges me. "We bonded over ice cream."

My nose scrunches up. "I'm far from pouting."

He hands me the leash and I want to tell him to keep it, but then it would look like I'm sulking. I take it with a smile before remembering I'm still wearing my fancy dress. One hand involuntarily slides down the silky material.

"You look beautiful in it, keep it on."

I hate that he suggests it, because I'm not ready to get out of the dress. I don't want him thinking I'm staying in it because he prefers it. Too tired to put up a fight, I slip my heels off, lowering a few inches before I slip on my Vans. I glance up at him, expecting to see a smug expression, but it's completely neutral, not giving away what he's thinking. I look back down, Skater shoes and a gown don't go together, but who's here to judge?

He opens the door for me and Griffin, but my dumb dog sits and waits for him to cross the threshold first.

"Why were you at the clubhouse that night?" I've been trying to recall every memory I have of that night and he's nowhere in it. How did I catch his attention, when I never saw him?

Max takes a step and pats his leg. "Come on, Brute." And lo and behold, my dog follows. I blow out a breath, walking in front of Max and bringing my dog with me to the street.

"You just talking to fill the silence, or do you really want to know?" He looks down at me. "I'm not a lying man, and I don't plan to sugarcoat the truth either. This is who I am, and I want you to know the real me because I'm not sure if anyone in my life really does."

I don't answer right away. *Do* I want to know? This seems like a situation where the less I know, the better.

Max surprises me by continuing to talk. He's not normally a talkative guy, but he seems to be in a good mood since I agreed to go home with him. "You have to admit, Griffin doesn't suit a dog like him. Brute is a much better name. Think of it like he chose his name."

I look to Griffin, then to Max, frowning. Griffin was a rescue and already had a name when I got him. "But he didn't, you did."

Max chuckles, matching my strides. It's Brute who's lagging behind with his huge size. "You sure are cute when you're trying to be spicy."

I stop at the end of the street, and Brute slowly catches up at his own leisurely pace with no worries in the world. Max places his hand on my lower back before the three of us cross the road.

"Stop distracting me. Why were you at the clubhouse?"

He removes his hand from my lower back. "I was there to kill your father."

I love my father, because he raised me, and that's what a daughter should do. It's hard to fault him for the things he's done, even forcing me to marry someone I didn't want to. At the end of the day, I've always hoped that if I went back home, he would protect me and prove to everyone it wasn't me who killed his best friend.

"Was that business or pleasure?" I joke, but his face stays serious.

"He was pleasure. It's the only reason I allowed myself to get distracted with you."

"What are you? What do you do, Max?"

He slides his arm up and loops it around my shoulder. The warmth cuts the night's edge and helps to keep me from shivering.

"I'm a butcher by trade. Most people in my world call me that by name and not Max. My brother is the Don of an Italian mafia family."

I close my eyes. "I traded a motorcycle club for the mafia. Awesome." My stomach turns at the realization that I went from one dangerous family to an even more dangerous family.

"My job is to make people disappear."

"Stalker, murderer, mafia, anything else on the résumé I should know?"

He's actually considering my question and takes a second to answer. "Loves dogs and kids?"

My face drains with blood. "Are you fucking kidding me?"

"Stop judging, it doesn't go well with that gorgeous face of yours."

I'm walking around in the middle of the night with a killer. This is how people go missing. Wait, technically, I *am* missing. I swallow, opening my mouth to respond, but he leans closer, his lips a few inches from mine.

"I can still see the judgment in your eyes," he whispers, the tenor of his voice rough and dark.

Our feet stop and I lick my lips, searching for the words before I ask, "What about the textbooks and saying you're taking classes? Was that all a lie, to be approachable?"

"Nope, it's all true. I like to learn and it settles me. I kill less the more I learn. Romeo, my brother, happens to think it's a very positive influence on my lifestyle." He holds my body tighter to his, like he's scared I'll run away. My body molds perfectly into his, creating this strange warmth that has to be the start to some dangerous illusion he's wrapping around me.

"Romeo?" Out of all of that, the word out of my mouth is his brother's name. I'm losing my mind. It has to be the explanation.

"Yeah, my older brother, the Don." The small voice in my head is yelling at me for not being more concerned, or scared, for my wellbeing. Instead, I want to know more about him.

"What do you do for your family?"

"I do a few different things. One of them is doing legal counsel for Dante's club, so when I said nothing will happen to you at Throne of Sin, you can trust me on it."

I'm getting distracted again. I need to focus on the fact he's a trained killer.

"Sienna, you're safe with me. I will never hurt you, and I will always ensure your safety. I promise." Brute lays down between us. "Look at me."

Hesitantly, I look into his eyes. They're warm, sincere, and have a way of drawing me in. My voice of reason, the one who has kept me safe my whole life, has, annoyingly, become powerless. This thing happening between Max and me is nowhere near *safe*. He stirs up too many emotions I can't put my finger on.

"I will never hurt you," he says again.

"Brute's tired. Let's go home." I sigh. This conversation is going to have to rattle around in my head for a while before I can process it.

I try to shake off Max's arm, but it stays looped around my shoulder.

Copy Cat

THEY LOOK CUTE TOGETHER. I've been studying Maximus Mancini for a long time now and I'm starting to think that the student has surpassed his teacher. Everyone slips in the end. Sienna is too distracting. He should be focusing on me more. Looks like I'm going to have to say hi to Sienna to catch his attention once again.

Chapter 14: Max

♥

I WALK INTO MY mother's house and slam the door behind me. She's been showing up unwanted to Romeo's house, spouting her nonsense.

Her eyes widen seeing my large presence and she runs to get her cross hanging on the wall.

"Don't you dare." I raise my finger and her hand pauses over it. "Dante and Savio may have let you beat them. I. Am. Not. Them."

She prays, her fingers moving over her chest. "You are going to Hell just like the rest of them," she angrily mocks.

I could say she is going there too, but I've learned not to engage with her religious antics.

"If you don't shut up, I'll place a bullet between your eyes." She sucks in a breath, knowing I'm a man of my word. I have no feelings for this woman. She left Romeo and me to survive on our own once our father was killed. She wanted nothing to do with us and didn't care if we became collateral damage in the mafia war. She was no better to my younger estranged brothers.

Hell, I forgot they existed for most of my life. I'm shocked they turned out as well as they did. I glance at my watch. This visit has already taken too much of my time. I have a house to blow up in the next hour.

"I've arranged for your mortgage to be paid for a year," I inform her, hating we're sharing the same air. My skin crawls with the need to get out of this run-down house as fast as I can.

"Is it true Savio is sleeping with the enemy? I'll pray for his soul."

I pinch at the bridge of my nose, unwilling to give her an inch regarding any of my brothers.

"Goodbye, Mother. This time, I'm the kind one. Take this as a sign from God."

I leave, hating that I even had to step foot here. I look around the crummy neighborhood, boarded-up windows staring back at me, lawns overgrown with weeds. If I was a regular person, I might have been scared to walk down the street.

I get into my car, seeing some teen boys eyeing my ride with tools in their hands, ready to steal my hub caps.

Hitting my Bluetooth, I squeal my tires out of the driveway. "I need confirmation on the wife. Has she left the house?" I ask of my surveillance team.

"The target is at home and the wife is out with her girlfriends. I have my eyes on her right now."

Sienna

MAX IS STANDING ON the corner of my street, watching my window. I spotted him the moment I waved goodbye to Dante. I pop a Cheezie into my mouth as we stare at each other. Once Dante disappeared, he stepped under the streetlamp and continued to look upward.

A light splatter of rain dribbles down my window, and I wonder how long he plans to stay out there. It's not like him to stand on the outside when it's just him and me. He normally makes himself at home, much to my annoyance.

My hand dips into the bag, finding it empty. I just ate an entire bag in one sitting, and it killed my craving perfectly. *Delicious.* My thumb dips into my mouth, sucking off the cheesy goodness, before I toss the bag onto the table.

He's still just standing there, like a madman. I worry something bad has happened and my heart wants to ask him about it, but I shut it down. Max is a bad man, and bad things happen to people like him. He knows where I am if he wants to make an appearance. Let's face it, he did what he wanted all the other times.

I change into my pajamas and slide into bed. It takes a few minutes to make the pillows perfect to support my back while I sit up and read.

I could call Max to see what's the matter.

It's unlike him, and I hate that my fingers hover over my phone, ready to pounce the moment I give them permission. No, he's a big boy who can handle himself. I put my phone down on the table and pick up my paperback.

The words jumble together, my focus shot. I haven't made it past the second page yet, despite my best attempts.

"You going to keep pretending to read that book?"

I scream and drop my book from the sudden voice. "I didn't hear you come in." My heart is going crazy from the scare.

"You never do." He smirks, but it doesn't reach his eyes. They're sad, in a way I've never seen before.

He walks in, picking the book up from the floor. "I can see why you picked this one. I like how the girl fell for her stalker," he says, handing me the paperback.

My cheeks warm at his observation. "I'm hardly ten percent in, I have no idea what this book is about."

"It took me a night to finish it. I liked it." He rolls his head and cracks his neck on each side. For the first time, I notice he has dark circles under his eyes.

I pat the bed beside me. He stays leaning against my wall, refusing to listen to my silent command.

"You okay?" I ask hesitantly.

His head lolls, looking like he's searching for an answer.

"It's too warm of a night to be cuddling Brute, so you might as well lay here until I fall asleep." Here I go, inviting the stalker into my bed. Some girls have no sense of self-preservation.

It's me, I'm some girls.

He steps forward, looking uncertain for the first time ever. He reminds me of a lost puppy you need to coax to come closer. "Might as well get comfortable. Take off the jeans and shirt."

Max's body freezes, his lips pursed, before he takes off his shirt. Sweet Lord, I've never seen a stomach as beautiful and toned as his. His hand begins to undo his belt, but his eyes stay on me, watching to see if I change my mind.

I lift the one corner of the covers for him as I wait for him to make it over to that side.

"Are you going to tell me what's on your mind?" I ask as he slips in beside me. Our skin brushes against each other, and it's like the oxygen in the room has been reduced by fifty percent.

My hands go to his shoulders and they feel like boulders. I give them a little pinch, trying to remove the knot.

"No." He tries to swat my hands away but, like him, I don't take no for an answer. "Shit, lady, that hurts," he complains like a big baby.

"Stop complaining and trying to change the subject. Tell me what's wrong. I don't stalk you like you do me, so I honestly have no idea."

He sighs, looking reluctant. "You don't have to invite me into your bed and pretend to be interested." He moves to get out but both of my hands pull him back in place.

"Max," I warn.

"I killed an innocent person today," he concedes.

My hands stop moving momentarily before I force them to move again. "Were you ordered to?" I question.

His eyes close and his back leans closer to me. "Nope, this one is on me. I fucked up."

The remorse radiating from him is felt in my every bone. I continue massaging his shoulders in silence. What else is there to say? I can't say I can condone it, but it seems like Max feels the same way. His shoulders never relax, even when my fingers begin to hurt from all of their work.

I can't help but feel bad for Max, even when he's the one who did wrong. "Tell me what happened." I find myself asking and meaning it.

"It was meant to look like a gas leak." He shakes his head, pausing. My hands rub at his back, allowing him time to continue. "I know better, it's not how I do things. The wife was supposed to be out with friends. I even had a visual confirmation, but in the end, it wasn't her. She was at home with the husband, and the house exploded too early, before I had a chance to make sure it was going to plan."

"This might not help, but we all choose part of our destiny." He turns his head, his eyes glued to mine, and it has me pausing, nervous to continue. My pulse speeds up, worried that I might be overstepping our little dynamic we have created.

I gasp when he tilts my face up toward his and turns his body to face mine. "Continue, I can see you want to say more," he murmurs, his voice soft in contrast to the grip he has on my hip with his other hand.

"She may not have done bad things like her husband, but I don't know a wife who doesn't have an idea of what their husbands do. She still stayed, enjoyed the lifestyle he gave her. Sometimes guilt by association is just as bad as the person actually committing the acts themselves. It's sad, and unfortunate, but 'innocent' is too strong a word." Max leans back and I release his shoulders. I think he might be made of part stone. "I get not being okay with it. It's moments like those that help define who we are, for better or worse," I add, before leaning back beside him.

It takes a while before his body begins to relax around me. Naturally, my breathing begins to match his and I drift off to enjoy the best sleep I've ever had in my life.

But when I wake, I'm tucked into my sheets and there's no evidence that he'd even been there the night before. I would almost think I imagined it, but his haunted eyes stay with me. My heart hurts for him and even in the soft light of morning, I wish I could take his pain away.

My hand checks my forehead to see if I have a temperature. It's neither hot nor cold.

Copy Cat

I DIDN'T SEE THIS coming. Max is getting a soul. He's going to be the perfect person to place all of our crimes on. I watch him, my lips curled in disgust. He used to be a strong man, one I admired and toured the country for. He's getting old, growing weak in his age. Pity. I'm almost embarrassed to say I once admired him.

Chapter 15: Sienna

❤

"**Y**ou'd be less stressed if you let me do the bookkeeping." I've been working for Dante for six months now, and Max and I are still doing this strange song and dance where he watches me from afar. He hasn't approached me since that night we shared a bed. I try not to take it personally.

Dante runs a hand through his hair, sighing while leaning into the chair's back from his once-hunched-over posture.

"You honestly want to be here beyond the hours you're already putting in? You make no tips with bookkeeping. It's like getting a demotion."

"But I'd be getting to use this beautiful brain of mine." I point to my head.

He's studying me, his eyes cautious. It seems not trusting people is a Mancini trait. I try to stay casual, not wanting to be too eager, scared he'll mistake it for anything other than me needing something to do with my free time.

"I'll give you three days to catch on. If it doesn't work out, don't be a chick and take it personally."

"When I'm better at it than you, don't go all manly and become brooding and fire me," I retort.

This brings a grin to his face and he points at me. "This is why I like you." He shuts his laptop and stands. "Savio, my brother, is having a fight tonight. Come as my plus one."

I cock a brow. This would be the second event I've attended with him. My thoughts immediately go to Max and I wonder if this would make him start talking to me again.

"Why?"

"You're in charge of the club girls and it's important they start seeing you as a step above, otherwise they'll never respect you. You're my right-hand woman now, and that job entails you coming to functions with me."

"When do we leave?" My chest blooms with pride. Dante is like the brother I never had. His words hit me in the middle of the heart. It might be the nicest compliment anyone has ever given me.

"Give me twenty," he responds.

T HE FIGHT IS LIKE nothing I've ever experienced before. Men are locked in cages and fight until one of them has to be carried out for their family to nurse them back to health. At least that's what I keep telling myself. Savio looks so similar to Dante, the only exception being the scars he carries with pride. Another realization hits...the Mancini men are ruthless and respected among their peers. I can see it in the eyes of others as they watch them, like they wish they were them.

The club girls were sent to Dante's house to prepare for the after party that Dante always holds after one of Savio's fights. Normally, I'm the one who is making sure everything is ready for the brothers' arrival, and I can't stop thinking of all the things I should be double checking, but instead, I'm here.

I peek at my phone, sending off another quick text message to the girls. "You ever stop working and enjoy yourself?" Dante asks, but there is pride in his tone. I bump his shoulder, not responding.

T HE CLUB GIRLS SEE me walk into the backyard and immediately turn their backs. *I'm not here to make friends.* I don't care what they think, but deep down, it festers, no matter what I tell myself. *This party isn't about me.*

I look up, seeing Dante on a large patio watching everyone below. I make my rounds, checking that everything was set up correctly.

People stand around on the brick patio and the lush green grass, mingling and drinking all the free booze like they are entitled to it. I've seen enough parties like this one to know how they go. I walk to the bucket of ice with all the different types of beer and grab some craft raspberry one with a grizzly on its can. The tab hisses as I crack it, before the cold liquid washes down my throat. Refreshing. Yet, I feel odd just standing here not doing anything, so I keep checking on the booze stock and everything else to keep busy.

"You're not special, you know." I turn to see one of the club girls. "You're dispensable, while us girls? Dante owns us, we're all investments, and here to stay."

She's glaring at me with hatred that I don't deserve blazing in her eyes. But I get it. They're all scared of what it means that I get to hang out with Dante, a privilege they all want and crave. I give her a large smile, showing my teeth, and her eyes flash with annoyance.

"Have you been liking your schedule?" She wanted to advance from waitress to dancer and I made that happen. She sucks in a breath, insulted I would hang something over her head. "I will take it away if you don't get out of my face."

This time it's my eyes narrowing on her. She turns on her heels and walks in the other direction. That's when my skin warms and I know Max is here. I search, looking for him on the edges of the party, but come up empty.

"Sienna..." Dante is standing behind me. "Come up, I want to introduce you to my family."

I finish moving the ice around in the bucket and wipe my hands on my hips. Suddenly, I wonder if any of them will recognize me as the girl Max was supposed to kill. *Would they finish the job for him?* Entwined with my anxiety, fear slithers its way deep into my bones and my heart rate accelerates. I really like my job and Dante; I'm not ready for it all to disappear from me.

Dante leads me through the house and up toward the balcony, my feet wanting to refuse each step. The souls of my shoes feel like they're cemented to the ground, every movement forced and needing more energy than the last.

"There's no need to be nervous. They'll love you." Dante tries to calm my obvious nerves.

I nod reluctantly, my skin chilling with the unknown. We step onto the balcony, and I'm instantly drawn to Max, perched in the corner, his face rigid, stone like. He doesn't smile like he normally does when he sees me.

"Congrats on your win tonight," I turn to Savio, opening up the conversation, hoping it will lead everyone's eyes away from me.

Savio nods his head, not saying a word. The silent type.

"This is Romeo," Dante introduces.

I raise my hand to shake his. He's staring at me, and my pulse speeds up. He knows. That's why he's staring and leaving my hand hanging. "Sienna. I'm the new bartender. Nice to meet you." I lower my outstretched hand.

"Likewise."

My hands fidget by running along my hips and back, looking for a pocket that doesn't exist. "And this is Max." I turn toward the direction Dante gestures. "He hates everyone, clearly the silent and brooding type."

Max's eyes flicker to his brother before they're back on me. It feels like everyone is watching our exchange.

"Hi Max." I hate the slow heat that rises from my chest and up my neck and force myself to turn, not wanting everyone to be able to read me like an open book.

"Once you get to know him, he's not so scary." Dante thinks I'm scared. My shoulders relax, knowing our secret is safe. I look up and find Romeo still assessing me. *He's* the scary one.

Cheers gather everyone's attention below, and one of the girls has taken up residence on a table and is shaking her hips. It's her signature move when she dances on stage.

"Want me to fix this?" I ask Dante.

He nods, running his hand through his hair. "Yeah, this isn't the place for that. Send her home."

I leave the balcony, the space allowing me to breathe easier. I'm better when I'm busy and have things to do. I head toward Tanya and pull her down from the surface.

A few people boo, but as soon as they see my serious face, they go quiet. Tanya tries to rip her arm out of my grasp, but I'm stronger. A cab is already waiting in the driveway by the time we make it around the house.

"Go home, sober up, and be ready for work tomorrow," I demand, walking her out of the party and to the front.

"Come on, baby, I'll take you home." A stranger walks up to us and tries to pull her into the cab with him.

I don't need this bullshit tonight. "I don't think so, buddy. Get the fuck out of here." I manage to get Tanya into the back by herself and close the door. Leaning toward the open front window, I give the address before taping on the roof.

"You're a cunt. She's a whore; I was trying to help her out."

"Then you should have paid for it at the club, but now you've insulted me. Don't bother showing your face for the next month. If you show up, you'll get your ass tossed out and another month added to your tally."

A rough hand is felt on my shoulder. I turn to give him more lip and a fist connects with my face. The impact has me stumbling back. The pain is instant and radiates all over my body. I can feel it at the tip of my toes and all the way back up.

I blow out a breath, my hand covering the sore skin. It's been a long time since I've felt this sharp pain of agony. I stomp my foot, hoping to distract myself from the injury. My hand moves from covering my eyes and I attempt to open them. My eye opens a crack, the swelling already taking over.

The man is no longer in my view and I step away, not wanting anyone to see me in this state.

"Who the fuck did this?" Max's dark voice rolls over me. His hands gently cup my jaw, his fingers feathering over my face as if he's scared to touch anywhere near my eye.

"I'm handling it, Max." My voice is soft and comes out weak.

"Whoever touches what's mine is a dead man walking."

My hands round his shoulders, and I can feel his barely-controlled rage in the way his body shakes beneath my palms.

"I want a name." He's searching the area, inspecting each person who's trying to go back into the house and away from his prying eye. His eyes are dark, wide, and have this blazing crazy look to them.

Without thinking, I kiss him. My lips cover his and it takes a few seconds for them to mold against mine. I kiss him with everything I have.

His hands cup my ass and pick me up, walking me across the yard until we're in the shadows of the house and a wall is at my back. His tongue strokes mine and I moan into his mouth, enjoying the sensation of his tongue and the way his pelvis rocks into mine.

His free hand slides up my hips and rests on my rib cage. I want Max to devour me and my legs wrap tighter around him as I lose myself to whatever this is.

He pulls away, both of us breathing hard, our chests pushing against each other. Our eyes are connected and the night's noises swirl around us, popping the bubble we created.

Second by second in our silence, my eye begins to throb harder. Max's fingers brush against my puffed skin, a pained expression shines bright in his blue irises. I've never seen so much emotion showing in his features and it has my heart opening more to him.

"Seeing you in pain has my insides going crazy with deep dark thoughts. I don't know how to deal with them other than being The Butcher," he drawls, his deep tenor vibrating through his throat.

I brush my lips against his. "This makes it all better."

He groans into my mouth and steps back, allowing my legs to slip down. Once my two feet are on the ground, he pulls his lips away from mine.

"You need to go home and ice this." I go to argue but he continues. "If Dante sees this, he's going to go batshit crazy and take it personally."

I don't want to draw more attention to myself over this. "Fine." His eyes flash with something unrecognizable and his jaw clenches.

It takes me a moment to understand why: I had only agreed once he brought up Dante.

A cab pulls into the driveway and Max leads me toward it. "Expect me tonight," he hisses, closing the back door of a cab. Disappointment sits heavy in my gut that he didn't get in the car with me. I could have asked him, and judging by the look on his face, I'm certain he wouldn't have denied me, but that would have meant he means more to me than he should.

I rest my head and close my eyes, my heart and mind confused. They continue to battle with each other, and I no longer know what's right.

Chapter 16 : Max

♥

I STAND THERE WATCHING Sienna's cab disappear into the darkness of the night. That kiss. She has a way of catching me off guard, and it thrills me to no end.

"We have a problem." Romeo smacks me on the shoulder and his car filled with his men slides up to the house. "Get in. We need to talk."

I can't deny my brother because he's the Don, so I mask my emotions and portray an indifferent, bored look.

We get in, the privacy partition already up. "What the fuck, Max?" He raises his hand like he wants to slap me. I steel my already-hardened features and glare at him, challenging his movement. His hand stays in the air, neither one of us saying a word.

"If you were not my favorite brother, I would kill you for lying to my face and disobeying an order. An order I gave you the *choice* to follow! Fuck man, you could have said no." Romeo's face is turning red, the cords in his neck straining. He's not used to anyone going against him.

"Then someone else would have taken the contract."

Romeo leans back in his seat and briefly closes his eyes. "What is she to you?" he asks, his hand brushing over his thick hair.

"She's mine," I answer without hesitation. "She's protected by me. Those fuckers are lucky I haven't killed them all yet."

Romeo curses under his breath. "When were you planning on sharing all of this with me? Dante is going to lose his shit."

"I'm telling you now. Don't ruin what Sienna has built at Throne of Sin because of me. Dante will be on a need-to-know basis, and he doesn't need to know."

"They're going to want retaliation." My brother's stress level is suffocating, and I watch as he rubs at his forehead.

"Want me to wipe them out tonight?" I ask, completely serious. My head is already buzzing with ways I could get away with killing an entire chapter of a motorcycle club. I probably couldn't do it tonight, it would take a day or two to set it all up.

"Killing can't always be the answer," Romeo stresses.

"But it's relaxing as fuck. Maybe you need to take it up, yeah?" His eyes grow wide with my asshole comments, and it's funny to watch his expression. He rarely shows emotion with anyone, but when it comes to us, we've been through too much together to hide it.

"If this backfires, you're taking all the blame." Romeo points a finger at me.

"It won't." I almost add on *I promise*, but I don't make promises. "This is one hundred percent on me. I'll say I acted against orders, which I did. If Sienna keeps working at Throne of Sin, no one will find her. She'll be fine. You'll be fine. And I'll be one fucking happy man."

"I must be in an alternative universe. Max Mancini in love. I never thought I'd see the day." My brother shakes his head in disbelief. He's staring at me like I have sprouted two heads and a magic tail.

Love? My face crinkles at the word. "Don't be jumping to conclusions." My forehead furrows deeper as I consider the word. "I don't know how to love." Love, what a weird word. It's hard to even know what something like that feels like when we were brought up in a loveless home. We knew order, discipline and pain. There's a reason our father was killed: nobody liked him.

"Are we done sharing? Cause I have a body to dismantle for hitting my woman."

Romeo rolls his eyes, his lips pressed tight. He doesn't like it, but he's used to this from me. "Make sure there's no evidence."

"I can do that for you."

I step out of the vehicle. The night's air smells fresher than it did earlier. My arms stretch outward as I bend my back, cracking it.

It's time to play.

B Y THE TIME I got to Sienna that night, she was fast asleep. She didn't even stir when I pressed a soft kiss to her cheek. I stared at the mark on her face, knowing death wasn't a fair punishment.

It's another two weeks before I'm able to set my eyes back on Sienna. Romeo made sure I was too busy to stay in town.

I watch her undress, changing into sweatpants and a hoodie, on my monitors. My cock hardens seeing her. Hell, just thinking about her these days has my dick growing into a steel rod. I use my phone to quickly send her a text and watch for her reaction.

Me: Wear the cute black ones.

She has this set that is shorts and a spaghetti strap tank with buttons lining the middle. It's incredibly sexy. I watched her cut off the tags a few weeks ago, but she hasn't put it on yet. Most nights she falls asleep with her clothes on, ready to run at first sound if need be.

She picks up her phone and her head snaps up a few seconds later. I lean closer, smiling at her reaction. Those gorgeous moss eyes search over the room. The moment she spots my cameras, her luscious lips pout and she walks closer. Her finger hovers over the small device and I wonder what she plans to do with it.

She walks over to her dresser and takes the requested clothing out. *Yes!* With a cute little wink, she holds up a finger and disappears from her room. I bite on my knuckle as I wait, my cock straining my pants.

My camera transitions to the other room, my eyes not leaving her. She has to climb onto her counter to get a large bowl down, and then walks it to her bed. She blows me a kiss before opening her bedroom window. *What is she doing?*

I'm intrigued. Her fingers fly over the screen of her phone as she texts me.

Mine: When did you plan on telling me about the camera in my bedroom?

Me: Did you honestly not expect it? Slip out of your hoodie, for yes you expected it, or take off your pants, for no.

Her frown is adorable. This girl has me wrapped around her pinky.

Mine: I haven't heard from you in two weeks, with no explanation, and you want to have phone sex? I don't think so.

Me: No, I want to watch you fuck yourself, but I'm happy with phone sex too. Would that mean I get to hear your sexy voice? You can call me.

She glares at the camera. That's when she takes the outfit I want into her hands. My lips hitch into a smile, and I say, "That's my girl." She stands, placing the clothing over her, as if testing to see if it would fit. She looks up, smiling at me through the camera, and points to the outfit. *Yes, Sienna, that one.* I lean back, undoing the top button of my pants to make room. My heart pounds in anticipation. That pajama set is going to look killer on her.

I swallow when I see her bring a lighter out and put the orange flame to the material. My eyes widen as I watch her burn it. The ashes and cloth fall into the metal bowl, which she'd placed under it.

This should deflate my erection, but it only grows harder.

She picks her phone up. **Mine: Guess neither of us will get to see that one. Me: I like you naked the best, anyway.**

Man, I love pushing her buttons.

Her hand slips under her baggy hoodie and it looks like she's cupping her breast, but I can't tell. My imagination is telling me that she is. She gets comfortable on her bed, the bowl between her legs, and her hand slips under her sweats.

Her hoodie slips upward, moving with her hand until I can see under boob. It's erotic, and I love it.

Me: let me see how wet your pussy is.

She glances at her phone but doesn't respond. I wait to see if she'll deny me. A few minutes later, she shimmies her sweats down to her ankles and I groan looking at that glistening pink pussy.

I unzip my pants and pull my dick out, stroking it. I have every intention of coming at the same time as her.

Her fingers dip into her cunt, and I want nothing more than to be inside of her. The feeling takes over me. I want to be the one touching her, making her feel good, making her come with my name on her lips.

Her eyes are on the camera as she strokes her swollen clit, and when her back arches and I know she's about to come, I explode onto my desk. Long, thick ropes coat the surface and I hiss her name at the same time she's calling out "fuck you" instead of my name.

I lean back into my chair, breathless, when I realize this feeling that keeps taking over me is me missing her. There's a reason I don't have many possessions. It's because you can't miss what you don't have.

Another week passes.

I used to rejoice when Romeo sent me out, but now I'm continually being drawn back here and it's all because of her.

I walk into Throne of Sin, nodding to the bouncer. Sienna's eyes grow large when she spots me. I'm bold and stroll right for the counter, needing to be close.

She looks around before her eyes focus in on me and stay there. She sucks in a breath and her hand over-pours the drink she's making and has her cursing. Her gorgeous green irises move back to her task, making the drink properly this time.

I lean my hip against the counter, watching. A light crimson floods her cheeks. She's a better bartender than this and I can't help the smirk that grows, because this is all for me. It's her reaction to me. I love it, crave it even.

Her light, floral scent twirls around me, and I have to fight against the urge to lean closer. At this rate I'm liable to jump over the counter and fuck the hell out of her. My dick perks up at the image I've placed in my imagination.

"Max, what are you doing here?" Her voice is low and her eyes dart around.

"I missed you." I've never said that to anyone. I don't miss people. "I've been thinking about that little moan you let out every time I kiss you and it has my mind wandering to other places."

"You can't say things like that here," she hisses, placing her drinks on a circular tray. She keeps her back to me as she talks to the other girls, ignoring me.

I have all the time in the world. I wait until she's done before I speak again. "Is this normal to have to wait ten minutes before being offered a drink?"

Her eyes narrow and her lips purse. It reminds me of a pucker before you blow a kiss.

"If you don't start to behave, I'll jump over that counter and kiss you. I will not tolerate you actively ignoring me."

"Dante isn't here," she hisses, making sure no one can hear our conversation.

"I know." I look her up and down, allowing my eyes to linger on every beautiful curve I want to kiss. "I came here for you. Did you miss me?"

She scoffs. "No." Her tone doesn't match the way her eyes sparkle when she's talking to me.

"Liar," I whisper. "I'm coming up tonight. Make sure to wear one of your cute see-through pajama sets." I wink, enjoying the way I fluster her.

"Hi, handsome." I look down and see one of the skeletons that work here and they ask, "Want a lap dance?"

My lips curl in disgust, my brow drawing up. "Not in this lifetime." I turn my attention back to Sienna, but she's filling more drinks while another girl stands waiting for them.

When she faces me, her face falls for a second and I spin around, eyeing the room. I check over my shoulder to see what caught her attention but see nothing. When I look back at her, she's looking at me with an odd expression.

"What's wrong?" I ask, feeling for my concealed gun.

"I was about to ask you the same question." She tilts her head, watching me.

"Your face changed," I respond. She's still looking clueless. Had I imagined it?

A firm hand squeezes my shoulder and Dante slides in beside me. He cups the back of my neck and drags me away from the counter. The only reason I'm allowing this is because I don't want to jeopardize Sienna's job here.

Once behind closed doors, I slap his hands away. "Why are you cockblocking me?"

"Those are my girls. Keep your dick in your pants. I don't want you messing with my business. If you need a date, I'll set you up on one."

"I find women like Sienna don't like my type of foreplay. I'll keep my hands off," I lie. I wonder what Sienna *does* like. I plan to find out very soon.

Chapter 17: Sienna

♥

I watch as Tanya, the table dancer from the party after the fight, offers Max a lap dance while licking her lips like he's her next meal. I pretend not to be paying attention to their interaction, attempting to busy myself with making drinks.

He hardly gives her a glance, and when he does look at her, his face is filled with utter annoyance. I relish his reaction, while she clearly flirts with him and refuses to notice his irritation.

I keep my face down, turning to grab a beer, but a laugh bubbles at the back of my throat until I swallow it, causing a rupture of fluttering in my stomach. Cracking the tab, I hand it over to Tanya, who's glaring at me, while I try to mask my smirk. Max looked at her like she was a small rodent he wanted to stomp.

Tanya is gorgeous, slim, great hair, big boobs; the men go crazy over her, but not Max. She looks disturbed that he refuses to give her any of his time, and doesn't quite understand it. I get that her personality is worse than watching paint dry, but he doesn't know that. In my experience, men only like so much personality and prefer looks over any kind of individuality.

Whatever the reason, my heart opens more to Max. My skin breaks out into a sweat as I realize that I like Max, my stalker, the guy who wanted to kill me.

I lift my arms, pretending to grab a bottle down from the high shelf to cool off my armpits, before looking at the thermostat. It's no warmer than any other day. *Get yourself together.*

The sound of a tray hitting the counter has me turning to grab the order held out for me. I try to focus, get my head back in the job, but it keeps circling back to Max.

Max places down a hundred-dollar bill for his untouched drink and shoves off the bar without saying a word. He meets Dante a few steps away and they walk out of the bar. My eyes trail them, and I'm left staring at the exit for a moment after they're gone.

"I thought I recognized you, Sienna." I spin on my heels, staring at a man who's taken a seat at my bar. "I know your pops quite well."

Up until a few months ago, I've never seen the man before, but he knows me. I recognize him from the dinner fundraiser Dante had me attend with him.

"Can I help you?" I ask, cautiously.

"I'm happy you asked, because you can, but I'll take a beer first." The man is lanky, but has enough muscle on him not to be a pushover. He has a square jaw and a crooked nose and eyes as dark and mean as they get. He doesn't smile, but when he talks, you can see his bright-white teeth that clearly could have used braces while growing up.

I grab a cold glass and push the handle for the draft beer. It sloshes over the side, creating a puddle around the glass when I hand it to him. He doesn't notice, his attention still on me.

"Who are you?"

"The name is Jameson." He smiles, showing his crooked white teeth. "You see, my cousin does a lot of business with your family's club, and it seems Dante has encroached on something of his."

"What does this have to do with me?" My heart is trying to fly out of my chest but I keep my voice even and my expression neutral.

"I need you to send off an email for me."

I stare at him, dumbfounded.

"An email?" I repeat.

"Yup, it's that easy." He swipes his hands together as if to say I'd clean my hands of him after this. Nothing is ever that easy.

"I send an email and then I never see you again?" I tense, not believing a single word he says, but I can't do anything about it. Hatred for my past life catching up to me steals my every thought. I glance around the establishment, despising the fact that I've been backed into a corner.

"Once that email is sent, I've never seen you before in my life," Jameson tells me with a wolfish grin. He'll keep coming back whenever he needs something and I know it. It's how these things go. I wish I was a stronger person who could ask for help, but I refuse to see any disappointment in Max or Dante's faces when they realize I'm not worth their time.

I rub at my eyebrow, pushing the skin in circles. *What's the harm in one little email?* This guy disappears for a while, and my family will have no clue where I am. I'll have fixed my problem.

"I'll go get the computer now." I sigh and push off the bar counter.

"Not so fast. I don't have the message yet, and I need to know I can trust you. Once I know you won't be going to run to Dante and tattle, you'll see me again."

He leaves his full beer at the table and walks out before I realize he didn't even pay for it.

"Sienna!" I shake my head at the sound of my name.

Two of the girls are waiting at the counter for me to make them drinks. "What is wrong with you today?" Shelby asks, eyeing me.

"She's upset she can't be on the floor like us girls. We see how you watch us with the men." Tanya flicks her hair and points to the orders. I really hate this girl.

I push down the nasty retort and make the drinks. My mind is swirling too fast to concentrate on anything. I'll deal with Tanya another day.

It takes me twice as long to make the orders, because I fuck up on two of them and grab the wrong beer. All these mistakes are cutting down on my paycheck.

Closing comes and Dante still hasn't shown back up. He normally returns late at night to walk me home. "Dante said for me to walk you home tonight, Sienna." I look up at the bouncer.

"Don't worry about it, Jerry. It's a two-minute walk, I'm fine." He looks unsure. "But if Dante asks, I'll tell him you walked me." A relieved smile hits his lips and he nods.

"I don't mind," he half-heartedly pushes.

"I like the quiet. You go home."

He nods, stepping out from in front of me, and I leave the building. I really do enjoy walking at night. I've done it my whole life and never had anyone mess with me. Tonight, there's a breeze in the air, which should have me wishing I had a jacket, but my body is too ramped up from the day.

Each street I pass, I have to retake in my surroundings. I'm completely lost in my head and don't remember most of my walk. I cross a few more streets before I realize I've gone one block too far. Sighing, I turn back, passing a homeless man sleeping that I hadn't seen the first time.

My building door is wedged open with a small piece of cardboard, allowing anyone to enter. *Stupid people.* I should get a shirt made up that says *I hate stupid people.* I kick it out, watching the door close behind me.

The overhead lights in the staircase flicker and the hallway isn't much better. Stopping at my apartment door, I grab for my purse that's not looped around my shoulder. My shoulders sag, realizing I forgot it in the back of Throne of Sin. What's wrong with me?

I rest my flat palms on the door before I allow my forehead to fall onto the wood. The small sound has Brute whimpering from the other side, and I hear his paw as it glides down the door.

"Forgot your key?"

I jump at the sudden voice and the hand on my shoulder. Max turns me. "Are you okay?"

I take him in, looking dashing in jeans and a tight white t-shirt that showcases all of his assets. Each muscle is perfectly carved into his body and it takes my breath away. He steps closer, leaving only a marginal gap between us, the close proximity increasing the speed of my breath.

His masculine scent wafts over me when he leans in, our bodies brushing against each other, to open the door. His lips feather over the pulse in my neck. "I love the way your body reacts to me."

My body is a traitor.

His hand slides down my arm and his fingers circle the pulse on my wrist before he moves his lips to it. "I never thought I would find anyone that captivated me more than the work I do. I find you exhilarating."

He effortlessly picks me up, tossing me over his shoulder, his hand smacking my ass. "I want to do bad things to you." His voice is deadly, but I'm not afraid. I know Max will never purposely hurt me. He won't even realize it when he breaks my heart. Even knowing this, a thrill shoots up my body, leaving my clit tingling and me wanting him more than ever. Tonight, I've become his prey and I'm going to allow him to feast on me, because I can't tell him no.

His warm hands leave my legs before my back bounces on my bed. Max is focused, much like how he gets when he's working on some math problem or reading his textbooks. A train could plow through the room and he'd still only see me. My arms are zip tied to the bedposts before I have a chance to voice any type of refusal, then my legs. I'm spread open at his mercy.

"I've imagined this moment since the first time I saw you." His eyes roam down the length of me and it makes me feel like I'm the most beautiful woman on the planet. "You are perfect."

He takes a knife from his pocket and it springs open with a flick of his finger. My eyes grow large seeing it, and my breath freezes with the rest of my muscles. The dull side of the blade trails down my neck, its metal cold against my warmed skin. It continues on its path until it stops at my shirt's neckline. Max tilts his head with a sexy smirk before his knife rips my shirt down the middle until the blade is past my breasts. The curve of my ample cleavage spills into the gap. With a small flick of his wrist, my breasts spring free for his viewing pleasure, and something flashes in his eyes a moment before he fists each side of my shirt and tears it the rest of the way open.

Max's features are filled with determination and there's a fire in his eyes I've never seen before. He looks like an obsessed man who refuses to accept he's lost his mind, but it's incredibly sexy. This side of Max is more of a turn on, because I'm the one igniting his passion.

Next, he cuts off my booty shorts, leaving me in my underwear. His hands tear the side of my full-bottom panties and a rush of cool air circles my vagina, stimulating my clit even more.

"Are you dripping for me, Sienna?" That voice is a low murmur of lust. No man has ever wanted me like this before. It shines through Max in a way that's intoxicating. I'm already drunk on him.

He pulls out a black Sharpie and draws something on my skin. I try to look at what it is, but I can't see it from this position. The thin, wet tip continues to explore my body.

"I'm marking all the pleasure and pain points on a body." His fingers skim my skin, touching me everywhere, while his marker creates a treasure map on my body.

"Where's the X?" I joke huskily.

"You're going to have to wait to find out." His one hand cups my heavy breast, it fills his hand and then some. My nipple is caught between two of his knuckles and the sensation of him squeezing my breast while pinching my nipple is mind blowing. I'm panting, wanting everything this man will give me. He lets go, his mouth latching on, and his tongue twirls around teasingly.

"Max," I purr, my hands pulling at the restraints. I want to touch him, feel him. His smile grows larger seeing me strain against the zip ties.

"This is all for you, Sienna. I'm going to worship you until you scream for me to put you out of your misery." He pulls out a delicate gold chain with little pink clamps on each end and dangles it in front of me. Nipple clamps.

"It will hurt before it becomes pleasurable." He informs, much like a doctor would before they do an operation. He's all matter-of-fact. I suck in a breath as he secures the first one to my nipple, and another quick breath as the other one is done. "The clamps restrict blood flow, creating this vibrant pleasure and pain feeling."

The pinching makes it hard to focus on anything other than my nipples. It takes a few moments before the pain fades and I'm able to watch him continue his worship of my body. I try to swallow the small, elicit moans that desperately claw at my throat to be released. The heat in his gaze adds a layer of excitement that has my pussy weeping for him.

Max is normally intimidating, but this side of him is alluring, powerful, and gray enough to entice my body to do anything he wants. He steps away to admire his handiwork and a chill replaces the warmth he possessed. His face goes out of view and I hear a drawer being opened and shut before my vibrator comes into view in his hand.

"Have you been imagining me when you touch yourself?" he asks, his deep voice laced with lust and sounding as sweet as honey. I refuse to answer, even after my cheeks warm and he snickers, my body having betrayed the truth. The stubborn side of me wants to tell him that drawer isn't for him to go through, but he turns the vibrator on.

The small purple device twirls and vibrates in his hand. He uses it to round both of my breasts and trail down my stomach before he dips it between my legs. It's touching all of my sensitive skin except my clit. I struggle against my restraints, wanting to move, to guide him where I want it. Teasing me more, Max slips it onto my inner thigh. He repeats the motion of in and out down my leg until he reaches the bottom of my calf and switches legs.

My hips automatically arch, trying to place my vibrator between my legs and on my clit. He continues this teasing, torturous game of his, and each time I arch, trying to get it closer to where I need it, he pulls it farther away.

"Max," I growl, the vibration rippling between us with the lethality of a ticking bomb that promises untold pleasure.

"Sienna," he parrots in a tender, intimate voice I've yet to hear from him.

My heart races with the same intensity as my clit. Each drum wanting—needing—more of what Max can deliver. The way he teases my body, I've never felt anything like this before, and my back arches, begging him for anything he might be willing to give.

He drops his ferocious gaze to my open mouth while his fingers circle my clit, hardly grazing it before two of them sink into me. He uses his thumb to hold my clit down while pushing two fingers in and out. I moan, closing my eyes at the same time.

"Yes," I pant, my breathing erratic. He pushes his fingers deeper and they scissor inside. Just as I praise him, he removes his fingers. My eyes pop open and my lips purse into an angry growl.

"Taste yourself." He places his two fingers at my lips. "Lick," he demands. My tongue darts out and I'm surprised by how sweet I taste. "Now suck," he orders. If it didn't sound so sexy coming from his lips, I'd refuse. Instead, I open my mouth like a good girl and he places his digits into my mouth.

I swirl my tongue around his fingers, sucking hard, trying to show him what he's missing. He pulls them out, inserting them into his mouth after.

His cock tents his pants, and once again, I pull at the zip ties, wanting to touch and tease him like he's doing to me.

"I can't wait to fuck these curves." I can feel his appreciation in the way his hands feather over my skin.

"Then do it."

He chuckles and shakes his head. "You're not ready yet."

He moves to the end of the bed, where I am fully open to him. "Fucking gorgeous." His head dips where I can only see the top of his hair, but I can feel his warm breath blowing on my vagina and clit. I feel a momentary flash of tongue against flesh before he's gone again, but never for more than a few seconds. He continues his teasing, one slow lick at the time. My hips continue to buck at his face.

The air hums around us. I have no insecurities or self-doubt, they cease to exist when Max is staring at me the way he does. My brain has turned into mush and only my body is able to think for me.

Flutters in my stomach ignite with anticipation, my desire for this man a flame burning deep inside the pit of my stomach. The rest of my body follows its cues, lighting up in a way it never has before. He uses one hand to hold my stomach down, effectively pinning my hips to the mattress, while he uses the other to continue squeezing my breasts.

"Max, stop playing like a boy and fuck me like a man," I huskily demand, my own voice sounding foreign to my ears.

His mouth latches on to my clit, sucking like it's his favorite popsicle, and his fingers unlatch the nipple clamps one at a time.

Pleasure and pain prickle my sensitive skin as his fingers fill my pussy. He fucks me with his fingers, my hips bucking like a bronco. My orgasm builds, starting in my toes slowly working its way up my body.

My head spins from the different sensations entering my nerves until I cry out Max's name as an explosion of pleasure erupts. He continues to finger fuck me, milking every last drop of my orgasm. I can't stop thrashing and moaning as the tidal wave crashes over me again and again, until my body goes limp.

The sound of his zipper joins that of my heavy breathing. No man has ever made me feel like this before. I can't even say I've felt an orgasm before, if this is what they should be like.

The bed shifts and I watch Max straddle my body. His cock is huge, thick, and throbbing. "Open that delicious mouth of yours."

I do as I'm told and he places the tip of his head at my lips. I give it a little kiss before my tongue darts out to lick it. Just the tip enters my mouth as I circle my lips around his shaft. His precome is salty on my tongue.

His movements are short and controlled as he straddles my face, and I suck his cock. I've never been in a position this vulnerable before. He has all the control and it turns me on. I *want* him to have this power over me.

The harder I suck, the faster his cock goes in and out of my mouth. It hits the back of my throat and I try to suck in air through my nose and relax my throat.

"Such a good girl," he murmurs. He fucks my face harder, his grunting moans music to my ears. "You are so fucking pretty like this."

I hum, enjoying the way he's dominating me.

"Do you think you deserve my cock in that tight cunt of yours?" I try to shake my head yes, but it's impossible in this position. I moan louder, trying to show him that I'm his good girl.

He pulls his cock out of my mouth and kisses me. As we kiss, his body moves over me and I have no warning before his cock slams into my pussy. He fills me entirely and it takes a few thrusts before my body is able to adjust to his size.

He fucks me hard, his hands holding on to my hips, his fingers digging into my flesh. It's firm and possessive. Each thrust has my body soaring, begging to climax again. I push back as intensely as he gives it. My clit brushes against his skin with each upward movement I make.

"I'm going to fill you with my come," he pants as he stares deep into my eyes.

"I'm not on any birth control." I quickly do the math in my head. "But we should be okay."

"Good. This will make you even more mine than you already are." He grunts and my head sways with all the endorphins and I don't give a shit about anything other than getting my next orgasm.

My hands strain to reach for him, held in place by the zip ties. "I love watching you struggle," he says before claiming my lips. The whole bed is moving with each thrust and I'm screaming his name again through our kiss as he pushes impossibly deep inside of me and grunts my name before filling me with his come.

He doesn't remove his dick from me the moment he's done. Instead, he stays nested inside and his forearms cage my face. "You are perfect, Sienna," he praises. He kisses both of my eyelashes before he places a soft kiss to my lips.

"Perfect," he repeats.

Slowly, as if it pains him, he pulls his cock out of me. Come still drips from his dick as he cuts off the ties on my arms and legs. My hands rub at the red marks on my wrists.

"Come on, let's shower." He walks naked to the bathroom, his ass sculpted just like the rest of him. On shaky legs, I follow after, my head still in the clouds.

The sound of water falling is already there when I step inside. Max has the curtain open as water cascades down his face. I close the curtain and quickly pee, a post-sex habit I can't see myself breaking. I flush, smiling at the sound of Max yelling when the water changes temperature, and wash my hands before stepping beneath the water with him.

I rub at the black lines on my skin, but the ink stains persist.

"It won't wash off because I haven't found X yet." He smirks playfully, his hands latching onto my hips.

Tilting my head, water sprays down on both of us. "Max, I can't wear my work outfit without people seeing all these marks."

He shrugs, not caring, and his eyes trail over my naked body. I try not to notice how large his hands are, and how rough they are compared to mine.

"Max," I growl.

"You becoming angry will only turn me on again," he warns, undeterred by my small protest. My palms push against his solid chest, and he's like a brick wall, refusing to budge. My forehead furrows with frustration as Max doesn't get it.

"How do you suggest, I cover these?" I scrub at the map with soap, over and over again, until my skin reddens.

Max's cock brushes against my inner thigh as he hardens. I look down at it and up at him in disbelief. He's getting turned on while I'm worried I can't go into work.

"I'm sure you'll figure it out. If not, I bought you long pants and a turtleneck."

I laugh at the suggestion until I realize he's being serious. The sound dies halfway in my throat as my eyes grow wide and my lips purse. "You're infuriating."

"And that's what you like about me." He leans down, stealing a kiss.

Chapter 18: Max

♥

SIENNA FALLS ASLEEP WITHIN minutes of me lying down beside her. I watch as her breaths even out and become steady, her face looking gorgeous and innocent of the corruption I will inflict upon her. I lie there enjoying her closeness, not wanting to leave her yet, but my brain won't shut off. It's like a drippy tap that keeps pecking, questioning what I'm doing with Sienna.

I slip out from under the covers and grab Brute's leash. I need a moment to clear my head and process what just happened here.

Fucking Sienna was like nothing I've ever encountered before. My heart is still pounding from the experience. I've never fucked a woman more than once, and all I want right now is another taste of her. I feel this intense protectiveness, more than just wanting to watch her. My chest hurts from this feeling.

I didn't think it was possible, but I'm in deep 'like' with Sienna. The emotion of that realization hits me square in the gut. It has my stomach dropping and looping as my heart sputters out of control. I never thought this would be possible. Could this be what my brothers spout on about? Is this love?

The way her body danced under me as her pussy choked my cock was like nothing I've ever felt before. Her moans and whimpers wrapped around my heart, pulling me in closer each time.

My hands itch to feel her curves under me again. Her ass and breasts fill out an outfit in a way designed to drive a man insane.

I speed up my walk as Brute stays a few leisurely paces behind me, even as I pull on his leash.

Sienna is it for me. There's no turning back now. I'm not sure she understands what that means fully, and yet, when our eyes connect it feels like she is part of my soul. Maybe I should go kill the entire motorcycle club. Then we can go anywhere she wants.

I'm so fucked when it comes to Sienna.

Brute and I round the block before making our way back up to Sienna. I stand in the doorway watching her sleep, my adrenaline going too crazy for me to sleep tonight.

I've never seen anyone so drop-dead beautiful.

I scrub my hand over my face before I grab a chair from the table and sit there watching her like she's the hottest movie on television. Once the sun has been up for a few hours, I take a break, only because I want to make her breakfast.

I easily maneuver around the tiny space as I make scrambled eggs. It's not her favorite, or anything close to it, but there's no oven to make cinnamon buns.

When I look up, she's standing there naked. She literally steals the air from my lungs. I freeze, my hand halfway to the pan with the eggs, unable to look away.

"What are you doing?" she asks, her hands constantly moving around her body.

"Feeding you." I force myself to stop staring at her curves and beautiful face. My hand shakes as I plate the eggs. "Put on some clothes." It comes out as a growl, but I won't be able to do as planned if she stands there naked a minute longer. I'll take her against the wall without any regard or restraint. Sienna deserves to be worshipped, not fucked by a man who has no control. It would be all for me. "Now."

She jumps and slams her door, placing a barrier between us. My heart is pounding against my rib cage. One look and my control snaps. *What is wrong with me?*

She comes out in shorts and a tank top, my map on full display. My cock is now fully hard and I have to adjust, but it does nothing for the pressure behind my zipper. It presses hard against it, strangling it uncomfortably.

"Where's the fork?" she asks, looking around at the table.

I lift the one in my hand and spear a piece. "Open," I demand, trying to get myself under control. Her brow lifts. "Please. I'm hanging on by a thread, trying to be a gentleman and not fuck you like a caveman," I confess.

Her expression softens. "That isn't the worst idea in the world."

I growl a response.

"You okay?" she asks, gently placing a hand on mine. Hers is so soft compared to mine. My hands are hard since I use them for work, and hers are delicate.

"No. My cock is strangling itself."

She fucking giggles. I want to growl more, but the lightness of her voice has me smirking instead. I sound like a teenage boy. I have it bad. I remember seeing my brother Romeo go through something like this.

I've somehow placed Sienna on my throne of obsession and I'm the one kneeling, ready for anything she might give me. *I'm a pussy, it's official.*

I feed her a few more pieces of egg while I battle my body to slow my pulse. The silence is comfortable, helping me relax. I take in a breath, inhaling her sweet scent. I remember it was her perfume that first gained my attention.

"What are you smiling about now?" she asks just before I place another fork full into her mouth.

"I like how you smell."

Both her eyebrows lift and she laughs. I lean back into my chair. Her hair is matted and she looks like she was just fucked. It's my favorite look on her.

"Now that I've eaten, when is it your turn?" she questions, wiggling her brows and slowly stepping away. This woman is going to be the end of me.

She slips the strap off her shoulder, then the other, allowing for her top to drop, revealing her tits. I stand, pushing the chair back before I stalk toward her. She laughs again.

I pick her up like last time and drop her on the bed for another round.

Chapter 19: Sienna

♥

"WHAT'S SHE SMILING ABOUT?" Shelby asks Tanya. Both are staring at me while I make their orders.

Tanya eyes me and shrugs her shoulders, not caring. With me being these girls' boss, I can't say they have warmed up to me. All they see is how fast I've risen and the favoritism they believe I get from Dante. What they don't realize is that Dante didn't save me like he did each of them. It was Max, and no one knows. Weird how my killer became my savior, and I'm okay with it.

"Sienna," Jameson is back at my bar. My eyes narrow and he slips an envelope over the counter with no regard for who is watching. I quickly snap it up, placing it in my back pocket while making sure no one has paid attention to the two of us.

"What's this?" I ask, the paper feeling heavy in my pocket.

"It's the message I need you to send."

I scratch at the back of my neck. What would my father's club do if they found me? "If I do this, I never want to see you again."

"That makes two of us."

He walks out and every fiber of my being wants to rip this envelope in half.

"Are you hiring?"

I startle, looking up. A pretty woman stands before me with long, dark hair. She looks sober, and nothing like the girls who end up here.

"Down the street is looking for a receptionist." I brush her off, but she refuses to have it.

Her shoulders square and she presses her stomach into the counter, keeping eye contact. "I didn't ask about down the street. I want to work here." She stares me down, a hard confidence reflected in her eyes and the firm set of her jaw.

"Why do you want to do that?" I ask curiously.

"I need the money. I'll work for tips; no other payment needed. I know how much a person can make working here." Her voice is strong and determined.

"Boss man will be in tomorrow. You can ask him then."

"Thank you. I'll be back." She rushes out and I hope I never see that girl again. She looks too innocent to work here. But who am I to judge? I'll let her fate rest with Dante.

I WAIT UNTIL CLOSING to send the message. Each press of the keyboard has my stomach twisting as I type the coded words. Nothing in code is ever good. I feel sick to my stomach about it and try to wash it away by quickly totaling the night's earnings. It doesn't help.

My mind is running a hundred miles an hour. I should have sent the message on a computer at a library. My muscles soak up my anxiety, tensing them into stone. This could easily come back to me or Throne of Sin. Fuck!

I glance at the unfinished bookkeeping. I'll have to finish that tomorrow before my next shift. Going to the computer, I log into the bank account and stare at the screen. Everyone needs a nest egg of cash, and after that message I could quickly become that someone. My fingers strum on the desk over and over in a nervous habit. What if something happens to Max? What if my family finds me? Again, that stupid message I was blackmailed into sending sits at the forefront of my mind. Dante won't even notice the pennies I'm taking. My stomach drops at deceiving my boss when he's been so good to me. He's like family, and family shouldn't do this.

My fingers tap on the table harder and faster. The only person you can be loyal to is yourself. I learned that at a young age. I was the one who had to look out for myself. My father taught me this lesson when he killed my mother in front of me for wanting a better life.

My fingers fly over the keyboard, making the small time-delayed transfers over multiple accounts. I'm only taking a few pennies an hour so it won't show up unless someone does the math, and I'm the one doing the books. I don't breathe easier, but I know it's necessary. I need a way to be able to survive if this job or Max disappears. I wish I was a better person, but circumstances have a way of blurring lines.

I finish up and close the computer. I stand there looking at the table. My stomach is still flip flopping. I wish I had the luxury of loyalty. Dante deserves someone like that. I blow out a breath, locking the office behind me.

Max is across the street as I leave Throne of Sin. I make my way to his side and we walk in silence. We both seem to be in our own heads tonight. It helps to ease the guilt that's sitting heavy in my gut. I'd ask what he's thinking about but I don't want him to ask me the same.

"My family is going to war and is going to need me around more." Max breaks the silence. "They think I'm still in Oakport Beach, living a hermit life."

"Who are they going to war with?"

Max takes my hand. He doesn't give me the impression that he's stressed over this. It's more like this is a way of life.

"The Bratva. My brother, Savio, fell in love with the Pakhan's daughter, and she comes with a throne of diamonds." I look up at Max, noticing he's more disturbed by this than the war.

"You don't agree with the union?"

We cross the street in silence and I almost expect him to ignore the question because it takes him two more streets before he speaks. "We grew up not under-standing love. We know how to follow orders and what happens when you don't. All of us have our own stories about the things we had to endure. Savio is putting it all on the line, and I'm in awe of the trust, I suppose."

That guilt I felt before slithers its way to my shoulders, sitting like a thousand pounds.

His fingers squeeze mine tenderly and a shiver dances its way down my spine when I ask, "Do you think you will ever regret not killing me?"

Max slips his hand from mine and pulls me into his side with his arm around my shoulders. "Life is too short for regrets. People spend too much time thinking and not enough time living."

His answer doesn't help.

Chapter 20: Sienna

♥

THRONE OF SIN IS crazy tonight. There's a buzz in the air that feels like mischief. The building is packed, way over code, and three police officers came in about fifteen minutes ago. I watch as they reemerge from the back after getting their complimentary private lap dance. They all wear smiles and there's no warning about any violations or tickets.

The girls are lined up waiting for their drinks, men are yelling their orders, and I can't keep up. I always keep up, but this is too much. The song *I Love Rock and Roll* blasts from the speakers. Shelby jumps onto the counter to dance, shaking her ass, even though we have a stage. She's in my way, her feet dirtying up my counter. I have to talk between her legs to get an order before I've had enough.

Taking the water nozzle, I spray her down. The men cheer as her white shirt goes see through and her dark nipples stand out.

"New girl!" I call to Demi, the girl who refused to take no as an answer to get a job here. She looks out of place, but she's a hard worker.

"Get behind here and help me out. I'll make the drinks, you can grab the beer orders." It's not like Demi is allowed to do much other than this, but this way she can be helpful. I'm not sure what Dante's angle is, but he's different with this one.

"Five tequila shots!"

I curse under my breath. I'm out of my two bottles and haven't had time to go get more.

"Vodka on the house and I'll get the tequila," I reply, quickly pouring the shots and running toward the back.

The music fades slightly as I make my way further from the bar. I open the door and step on the first shelf, going on my tiptoes to reach the bottle I need. Two hands cup my ass and I shriek, losing my footing. It's not like anyone can hear my scream over the noise of the bar.

Strong arms catch me, putting me at Max's mercy. He holds me at this impossible angle, my feet unable to right themselves. My entire weight is being held up in his arms.

"I like you vulnerable like this." He bends down, kissing me. My arms naturally wrap around his neck and ever so slowly, he places me on my feet, all while we kiss.

"I hear that my brother asked you to be his plus one...again." Jealousy laces his tone.

"This works best for you. I know you like a chase," I tease Max.

"It's a good thing Demi showed up to distract Dante. I'm not sure I would be able to stay silent knowing you hold all his attention." I go to explain that this is not the case, but he covers my mouth. "I know, I know, you're friends. Best friends. I don't have to like it, but I accept it. You're here because of me after all."

His hand trickles up my skirt, tracing the hem of my panties.

"How about I show you how much you mean to me?" I say seductively, my fingers walking up his chest before I cup his solid pec and grasp his growing package with my other hand. "When I'm not slammed at work."

I push off of him but he pulls me in closer and his fingers slip past my underwear to circle my clit.

"It's busy out there," I half protest.

"And the only way you're leaving here is if you're a good girl and come on my fingers," he murmurs in a low, gruff voice. His fingers enter me and his thumb presses on my clit.

"Max, seriously, I need to go back." I swallow the moan that wants to bubble up from my throat as he stares at me with such wonder and desire. I'm not sure I'll ever get used to someone looking at me like this. The feelings he elicits from me are terrifying. I fear my eyes reflect equal parts lust, trust, and only a tiny part of the annoyance I'm desperately trying to cling to.

"And you will." His fingers twist, drawing a moan from the back of my throat. His eyes hold a determination I've come to recognize. He kisses my neck and my body relaxes as I force myself to focus and enjoy the moment. This is happening no matter what I say.

My neck curves as he makes his way from the bottom of my ear to my chest with soft kisses. His other hand plucks at my nipple covered by my shirt.

"My perfect, needy, Sienna." My head falls back, enjoying the way he makes my body come alive. All thoughts about the bar float away and Max is the only thing that consumes me. It should be worrisome how fast he can make me forget everything, and the way I allow him to consume me. No one has ever held this much power over me. I shiver involuntarily and heat spreads through my belly, right to the apex of my thighs.

I arch my chest into his hand as pleasure ripples through me. Waves of hot, delicious, lust wash over my nerves but it's not quite enough to push me over the edge. I grind my hips harder against his hand.

"I love when you become my slut." He sucks on my earlobe, his stubble brushing over my cheek.

I'm desperate for my release, grinding shamelessly.

"Tell me you're mine." There's an edge to his voice, but when I look into his face there is tenderness.

I refuse to answer, scared that if I become his, then I'll lose myself entirely. He bites on my lower lip, showing me his displeasure when I refuse. He licks the pain away, murmuring, "If you want to come, tell me you're mine."

I'm breathless, squirming, and starting to sweat, each breath bringing me closer but never close enough to come apart.

Max plays the slow game, stroking my clit, seeming to have all the time in the world.

He bites down on my neck, making me gasp. "I'm your slut."

He flicks my clit before dipping his fingers into my wet pussy, dragging the wetness to where he wants it. My pulse is flying. My body is shaking. I don't know if I can take much more.

"Max," I plead, not knowing what I'm asking for.

"Come for me," he demands in his husky, sexy voice. His thumb brushes over my clit, back and forth, as his fingers fuck me like his cock would. I'm panting, my breath unable to recover, and my heart is beating erratically.

His lips suck on my neck as my head becomes light and I'm moaning his name. Light flashes in the back of my eyes as my body spasms in his arms. Coming down from the high, I watch as Max places his fingers into his mouth, sucking my juices off them.

Three bangs on the door and the handle wiggling has the flames of my arousal fading like someone threw a cold bucket of water on me. "Shit," I curse.

"Sienna?" It's Dante's voice coming from the other side.

"You okay? Why is the door locked?" I glare at Max but he looks like a kid in a candy shop. I grab the bottles just before the door opens.

Max slides behind the door and holds a finger over his lips where Dante can't see.

"It must have fallen locked when it closed on me. I had to climb the shelf to get these." Dante studies me, cocking a brow, looking like he doesn't believe a word I'm saying.

"I've been sitting here waiting for someone to realize I went missing." I shove past him, heading toward the bar. Dante is at my heels, but stops when he notices Demi behind the bar. I look behind me and he's stomping toward his office now.

I look back at the new girl, wondering what the fuck that is about. I don't have time to think further as I rush back.

"What happened to you?" Demi asks.

"I got locked in the storage room."

She walks up to me and her hand touches my neck. I try to swat her away but she's withdrawn before my hand reaches my neck.

"Did you have to wrestle a vacuum too?"

Before I have a chance to respond, she's going back to her section to waitress.

"Fucking Max," I grumble under my breath. Of course he would mark me. I'm off kilter the rest of the night. I keep thinking everyone is staring at my neck, wanting to ask questions, but I know these girls. If they thought the same thing too, there would be comments.

·❤·❤·❤·❤·❤·

I LEAVE FOR THE night, staying on my side of the street and refusing to make my way into the shadows where I know Max is lurking. I stay in the light as much as possible, and it takes three blocks before Max crosses to my side.

"I'm not talking to you right now," I say sourly.

He chuckles, igniting my anger. "I'm sorry," he apologizes, but his expression doesn't match his face.

I stop and stare at him. "No, you're not." I keep walking.

"You're right. But I am sorry you are angry. I got jealous. Dante was going on and on about how awesome you are and how you are the perfect plus one. I couldn't help myself. I pride myself on control, and you are the only thing or person to have me unravel."

"What would I say if Dante noticed the hickey on my neck? Or walked in when your fingers were in me. Throne of Sin is my place of work. That can't happen again."

"Dante has his head so far up his ass he would never notice. You're going to start seeing me there more." He grabs my hand, entwining our fingers, turning me into his body. "I'm going to have to start getting to know each of the girls that work there. I'm telling you up front because I don't want you to get jealous when I have to flirt with them."

He's not turning this around on me. No way. "Do I flirt with Dante?"

"He doesn't stop talking about you."

"Answer my question, Max." This time it's me staring him down, but it doesn't unnerve him like it does when he does it to me. His fingers brush a piece of hair behind my ear.

"You're beautiful when you get angry."

"Max," I growl.

"He's lucky Demi has come into his life, because I hate when he talks like he knows you better than me."

"Whose fault is that?" I ask.

I watch his Adam's apple bob as he fights to force his emotions away. This is the most real I've ever seen Max. My anger melts slightly seeing how hard he's fighting to become emotionless but can't.

"I will try to do better, until the day I can claim you as mine in front of everyone," he concedes. He presses his lips to my forehead. "Please forgive me for becoming a caveman and only thinking with my cock?"

A small smile wants to tug at my lips but I force it down. Max needs to see how serious I am.

"Please," he begs. A moment passes, because I don't want to give in too easily. "If I have to fall to my knees, I'll be forced to worship you on these streets for everyone to see."

I playfully swat at his shoulder. "I forgive you. This time."

He links our fingers together, as we continue the walk to my apartment.

Chapter 21: Sienna

♥

"Hey Sienna," Dante calls for me as I walk past his office. "Come here."

I walk into his personal space having only been invited in here a couple of times. He has a cupcake in his hand, which is outstretched toward me. I look at the small, single candle flickering on top.

My forehead ruffles in confusion. "What's this?" I ask.

I glance back at Dante. He looks relaxed and far too happy for it to be his natural state.

"You never told me when your birthday was, so here's a cupcake to celebrate your anniversary here."

The gesture is so thoughtful, it warms my heart. After my mother died, I haven't had cake or anything like that on my birthday. Not that today is it, but it's moments like these that have me wishing this could be my real life. One where I'm not constantly looking over my shoulder, expecting something bad to happen. Dante has me feeling like we're real friends, and I've never had one of those before. The closest thing to a real friend I had was Ginevra, and we had to hide our friendship because of who my family is.

At the clubhouse, girls were forced to play with me because of who my father is, or the opposite, they weren't allowed to play with me because of who my father is. Then I got to be a certain age, and when I looked around, I had no one.

"We don't need a reminder of how much you needed me," I tease, trying to downplay how much I appreciate this act of kindness.

He gestures his hand for me to take the sweet, and I blow the candle out.

"You have to eat half." I'm already ripping it in two before he has the chance to deny me.

I hand him back his part and we both sink our teeth into it. The outside, and part of the inside, is made from real whipped cream. The smooth, creamy taste slides down my throat and now I regret sharing with him. I'm done with mine in two bites and wish I had a hundred more. Its death-by-chocolate taste is my favorite.

"Here's the rest of them." He brings up five more in a clear plastic container.

My mouth waters at the thought of having one more. "Thank you, Dante."

He steps up and gives me the container, but I steal a hug. He stiffens in my embrace and holds his breath, only releasing it when our bodies are no longer touching. I had hoped the viewing area might help him with his no touching rule. I'm not sure if it has.

"Don't share with anyone, they don't deserve them, and I don't want them to start thinking I'll buy them cupcakes for anything they think needs to be celebrated."

"I would never dream of ruining your broody, dangerous vibe you wrap around yourself like a security blanket."

He lifts a brow and I laugh at his less-than-humorous expression. He loves it when I tease him. I give him a small wave before closing his door and making my way to the back room. I open the container and inhale another cupcake. It's still as good as the first one. I suck on each finger, cleaning the small amount of whip from them before hiding the cupcakes until I can take them home.

The evening is unnaturally slow. Dante had me cut a few of our girls for the night, which never happens. I have time to do some of the book work at the bar and clean out the back room. It's never been so organized. Each time I go back, I enjoy another one of my cupcakes. Just the thought of them has me smiling.

"I'm going to toss this in the trash." I let one of the waitresses know, lifting a garbage bag in her general direction before I head out the back.

The light that normally shines bright flickers intermittently at best, making the area dark. I scrunch my nose while looking at it. I'll have to let Dante know about this tomorrow.

Walking toward the dumpster, I toss the heavy bag in while keeping the lid held open. I hear feet shuffle in the darkness and I let the lid drop with a heavy bang before turning to run back in, but a pain-filled moan has me pausing.

I should get the bouncer to come back here, but instead, I walk toward the sound. I recognize the outline of Max instantly. The light flickers and his face looks hard, possessed, and intent on killing the man dropped to his knees at his feet. Max sucker punches him in the gut before kicking his jaw.

I turn my head and a small, muffled squeak slips through before I can hold it in. The last time I saw rage like that was when my father put a bullet in my mother as she tried to run away. My father's face at that moment in time flashes through my mind, the same cold hatred had shone in his eyes as well.

My body freezes, locked in place as the flashback runs through my memory, immobilizing me. The realization that I've exchanged one gilded cage for another sits heavy in my gut.

"Sienna." I turn at the sound of my name. Max's eyes are large, not expecting my interruption. Vulnerability flashes in his deep-blue irises before they fade and become lifeless.

"This is who I am, Sienna." The sound of a bullet leaving its chamber has me jumping back. My mouth drops open as the man slumps to the ground. I'm forced to remember that this is what Max is; a killer. I was supposed to be on the receiving end of one of his bullets too.

"I can't change who I am. This is in my bones; I thrive on this need too much to change. The honest fact is that I love my job." His words are distant, vacant like his soul.

"Why did you kill him?" I'm still in shock, or disbelief, that he killed a man in front of me.

"He was a dead lead on who's trying to hurt Savio's woman." There's no remorse in his expression. He's not even fazed by the dead guy on the ground while I can't stop staring at the body. Someone could come back here at any time and see, but Max is only watching me, unscared of the consequences.

"What were you looking for?" I ask, tilting my head back to him. The messed-up part is that the tiny voice in my head isn't telling me to run. Instead, it's telling me to dig deeper into Max.

He steps closer, kissing my forehead. "Just some cyber bullying. Nothing of concern. I protect my family at all costs."

Is he inferring that I'm his family?

He leads me back to the door, his hand on my lower back. I'm still trying to process what's happening and I allow for him to take me back inside. The door closes with finality, me being inside and him staying outside. I lean back against the door, the image of Max shooting the man playing on repeat.

Chapter 22: Sienna

T HERE'S A SINGLE ROSE at the base of my doorway when I push it open, the once-perfect bloom now destroyed with a few petals falling off from the pressure of the wood running over it. I freeze seeing the flower I've come to despise since I was a little girl. Its green thorny stem has a little water container at the bottom to keep it fresh. I want to pluck each silky red petal and toss it in the trash; instead, the color, the smell, and its sharp green thorns have me pressing my thumb against it until my skin breaks.

I look around the vacant hallway for a clue as to who dropped this off before bringing it inside and placing it in a cup on the table. It must have been Max. It's not Max's fault he doesn't know I hate roses. They were the flowers on my mother's coffin.

You would never know it was my father who put a bullet in her by the way he spared no expense on her funeral. He played the grieving husband perfectly, even though her casket was empty. The official report says she's a missing person, presumed dead, and her burial plot lies empty.

I prefer sunflowers. It's what she and I would always plant. We would steal the seeds from my father's favorite package of Spitz and sometimes from bird seed packages if we had any, but once they grew tall enough, he cut them down before they beautifully flowered, calling them weeds.

With a smile on my face, I remember the one time my mom and I got one to flower before he found it.

I sigh, thinking about all these tainted memories. I will never go back. Here, I have no sleepless nights. I'm not forced to be someone's pawn.

Along the way to work there are a few more roses scattered on my path. I want to ignore each one, but my feet refuse and I pluck each one up. My thumb brushes over a thorn, the sharp protrusion scraping at my fingertip.

I place them behind the counter in a glass and continue to the back. I'm the only one here, everyone's shifts start later in the day, but I need to do the schedule, place the new girl, Demi, on a dancing shift and decide who will lose a dancing shift for a waitress shift before ordering inventory.

I sit in my chair and stare at the computer, the guilt from stealing money still heavy on my conscience. I need a safety net, but it feels wrong to do this to Dante. It's not like I can return it now. I can only imagine how that would go. "Hey I stole a bunch of money." *Pop, pop, pop.* There I go six feet under.

Eventually, voices make their way back to the office I'm in. I'm shocked to see the few hours I had disappeared. Most of the girls are on the floor while a few others trickle into the staff changing rooms. A rose sits on the counter for me. My eyes automatically search for Max. He and Dante are having a hushed conversation, but it looks heated from their body language.

I pick the flower up, smelling it, and my nose wrinkles involuntarily. Wanting to mess with Max, I leave it on the counter, waiting for him to make a comment about it.

Looking back up, Dante is shaking his head on the way to his office while Max strolls toward me. "Hey, pretty lady. Looks like I'm going to get to look into your gorgeous eyes every day now," he flirts, smirking at me with his eyes shining.

He leans on the counter, lowering his voice, and asks, "You know much about Demi?" His eyes narrow on her, his face hardening.

"She's a nice girl, hard worker. Don't you dare scare her off, Max."

His hand flies to his chest. "Little ole' me? You watch, I'll have her eating out of the palm of my hand."

I chuckle as I watch him try to transform himself into something he's not. It's not working, he's still intimidating as fuck.

"Leave the girl alone." I shake my head.

"You and Dante sound far too much the same." He takes a seat and I give him water. "Can I have a beer?"

Crossing my arms over my chest, I say with a playful attitude, "Beer is for paying customers."

He grabs my hand, staring into my eyes with a serious expression. "Be my date this weekend."

"Not a chance."

"I'll have to ask someone else then."

I can't help but laugh, and his lips purse at my reaction. He looks so damn sexy when he frowns.

"Max, I'd love to go on your arm, but have you checked this over with Dante?"

"I don't need my brother's permission to take my girl out," he grumbles, his voice rough with possessiveness.

"Does *he* know I'm yours?"

His face drops, and I have my answer. "I hate you being his date," he pouts.

"I'm not his date." Shock resonates across his hardened features. "Demi is."

"She must have one magical pussy." He steps away from the counter and goes straight up to one of the other girls. I'm not worried one of them will be his date. Dante has a strict business-is-business rule, and up until Demi, he has refused to mix pleasure and business when it comes to his club.

Even knowing this, I can't help but keep my eye on Max as he talks to each and every girl here. *What is he doing?* "Careful Sienna, people might start wondering why you keep eye fucking me," he teases as he walks past, winking at me. He disappears into Dante's office and the two of them leave together a few minutes later.

Not even an hour has passed when I get a phone call from Dante telling me to cut Demi. I look around and we're busy enough to keep her. Before Demi showed up, I had never cut a girl early from their shift. She's not going to like this, but he's the boss.

"A FRIEND OF MINE died because of you." Jameson sits at a stool in front of me.

I look around to catch a bouncer's eye to toss him out, but none of them seem to be around. "You're not welcome here," I hiss, my heart rate rocketing.

Fear of having to go back to my old life slithers its way down my spine. My entire body tenses and I feel helpless once again. I've come to loathe this sensation, and hate how much I'm liking this new life I've been creating.

"Before you kick me out, look at this." He holds up his phone and there's a video of a little girl on the screen. I have no idea who she is, but it plays on my heartstrings because I can't help but think of myself at that age. I take a steadying breath, my stomach twisting violently at the image.

"This little angel is going to be important to your boss. I have a man who has her at the end of his scope, if you're catching my drift. If you don't do as I say, she dies." He holds his fingers in the shape of a gun and moves them like he's shooting something.

"What do you want?" I grit my teeth, bile rising in my throat. I'm a sucker for little kids.

"I need you to come to a function as my date and introduce me to Dante as such."

I want to say no, but looking at the little girl stills my tongue. Defeated, I reply, "Fine. But if you ever come near me again, I'll be sending the Mancini men after you."

"They have never scared me before, but you can try," he taunts. "Just remember, that little girl's life is in your hands."

If I go to Max or Dante, I'll have to come clean with everything I've already done. I'm trapped with no escape. It doesn't matter where I go. It's like Jameson knows this with that shit-eating grin he's giving me.

He walks out of the club and I wish I could do something, anything, to change this path I've been set upon.

MAX WALKS INTO MY apartment behind me after my long-ass night at work. Neither of us said a word on our way home. I think he's still ruffled that I said I wouldn't be his date. It's going to look extra bad now that I will be attending with another man. I can only imagine the conniption he's going to have.

I want to tell him about Jameson, but I can't have another death on my conscience. I place the bouquet of roses on the counter before changing into my pajamas, forgoing washing my face.

As I'm pulling my shorts over my hips, I realize I've been sleeping in my clothes less and slowly beginning to wear PJ's. It stumps me for a second before I toss my shirt over my head and replace it with a silky soft one.

Over my shoulder, I glance at the roses on the table. Max hasn't said anything about them, but he keeps eyeing them. They're the first thing he's given me and I don't want them to die, even if I don't necessarily like them.

Reentering the small room, I grab the roses I've gathered throughout the day and place them in the cup with the other one.

"Roses," he grunts, finally commenting on them. "I thought sunflowers were more your thing," he says absently, bending down to rub Brute. Brute doesn't even get up to greet us anymore. It's like he knows I'm safe so he can have time off from his guard dog duties.

I never told Max I love sunflowers. How would he know? "They are. I would never buy roses. I don't even like their smell." I'm too tired to sugar coat my feelings.

"Then why are they in your house?"

"I didn't want to hurt your feelings." I go back into my room and Max follows. The bed is calling my name and I slip under the covers.

"Why would that hurt my feelings?" he asks, his arms crossed over his chest.

"Because you went through the trouble of hiding them all day long."

I close my eyes, but my pillow isn't feeling right. I smack at it with my hand a few times, trying to mold it to how I like.

"If I were to buy you flowers, I'd have bought you a hundred sunflowers, not a few half-dead roses."

I lift my head. "What?"

"Those flowers aren't from me."

My heart stills and my eyes widen as I process his words. Fear slithers through me as I realize maybe my family has finally found me. Max is giving me a quizzical look now.

"I'm tired, Max." I try to hide my fear and close my eyes. My mind is reeling with what this means. I wait for him to argue with me, but he doesn't. Like most nights, he shuts off my lights and the space beside me dips. His strong hands pull me in, embracing me.

"You're safe," he whispers. That rough voice of his and the way he holds me is enough for my body to relax into his. "When I find out who is sending my girl flowers, I will destroy them. I will do it for you." I wish his words sent me into a panic, but instead, they give me comfort.

Chapter 23: Sienna

"YOU CLEAN UP WELL, for being a bar wench," Jameson says as we walk into the gala. *Who says things like that?* He holds on to my elbow tightly, the pressure of his grip painful, but I refuse to wince.

My eyes seek out Dante, finding him with his whole family at a circular table. Max is there with a date, as promised. My lips twist with disgust, even though I have no right to the reaction. Jealousy ripples through me. They all look happy, like a family unit. I never had that and wouldn't even know how to fit in.

I wonder if Max realizes how easily he fits in with them. The men stand, leaving the table and making their way to the bar.

"Now is a great time for introductions." Jameson pushes me toward them, staying behind and out of harm's way.

I force my shoulders back and hold my head up high as I approach them. My heart is pounding against my ribs and I swear they'll take one look at my face and see guilt. No one notices me, except for Max. His eyes are glued to me as I take each step. They blaze with anger and lust, the combination lighting my skin on fire and my heart adopts an impossible pace.

Max in a three-piece suit is heavenly. His broad shoulders stretch his jacket in all the right places. His smirk grows when he sees me looking him up and down before my eyes turn to Dante.

I was hoping Dante would spot me right away, but the conversation with the brothers has his complete attention. I pause, wishing I could turn back. I glance back to Max, his features are hard seeing my attention turned to his brother.

Taking a deep breath, I force my presence to be known. "If you're not ordering a drink, move on so others can," I say in an annoyed tone, but the smile on my face can't wait to see their reaction to someone talking to them like that.

As expected, the four Mancini Men turn to glare at me, but when their eyes land on mine, their faces melt and smiles curve their lips. All but Max's, of course. I step in to give Dante a hug, just because I hate the way Max is looking at me. Dante stiffens in my embrace but after a second, his arms relax into a hug around me too. It's progress.

"Babe, when you said you couldn't come with me tonight, I asked someone else," Max cockily responds.

"Yes, I met her earlier. Lovely girl," I lie. I already hate her for no reason. I turn my back so Max is no longer in my view and speak to Dante. "Dante, I want you to meet *my* date."

Dante extends his hand to the tall stranger behind me. "Not him." I roll my eyes and this time it's Max who lets a laugh escape his frown. "He's over there." I point at Jameson and hold my breath, not knowing what reaction any of them were going to have.

Dante's face instantly transforms into something I've never seen. It's pure rage, his hands curl into fits until he notices everyone staring at him and he masks his emotions. *What the hell have I gotten myself into*?

I take a few steps back when all of their attention slides to my date, wanting to get away as fast as I can. Max and his brothers grumble something under their breaths, before I've turned around and walked in the other direction. I don't care how sketchy this might look.

A hand grabs mine, and before I can rip my fingers away, Max turns me to face him and pushes my back against the wall. His arms fall to the wall space beside my head as he leans down into me.

"What have you managed to tangle yourself in, Sienna?"

Max

Sienna is frozen, pushing herself against the wall like it will suck her in to free herself from me.

"How did you manage to be a naughty girl when you've been everything I watch and think about? You're making play moves from under my nose while I'm the one who can't get enough. I watch you eat, breathe, sleep." I can hear the vulnerability crack in my voice, and it makes me feel weak.

"You need a hobby." Her voice is breathless caged under me.

My nose slides down the side of her face until my lips are at her ear. "You *are* my hobby." She's way more than that.

I've never slipped until Sienna came into my life. An unhinged feeling coats each of my nerves while she masks her emotions and whatever she was struggling with before disappears like she's transferred it all into me. The dread that was so obvious in her eyes has now transformed into determination. My strong girl is back.

My normal numb heart is aching, but it doesn't even know why yet, and I can't stop looking at her.

Her fingers brush over my jaw, the electricity between us zapping like a taser, digging deep into me, and I'm tethered to her, unable to let go. I'll never let her go. I'm in love with every side of her, even the part that defies me. It has my heart rate accelerating, my muscles becoming excited about the chase she's going to lead me on.

"You need to let me in." My lips brush against the shell of her ear. "It would make this so much easier." I smirk and look at her face. "But I've always liked a challenge."

She has this knowing gaze as she looks up at me from under her dark lashes. "Where would the fun be in that?" she purrs with a sexy intent that has my cock hardening.

My eyes drop to her lips and she shifts her body weight but makes no attempt to escape the way I've pinned her in. Sienna's breathing quickens, her palm landing over my heart. My fast beats thunder under her touch.

"You feel it too," I say. It's not a question but a statement that has her giving me that shy grin of hers. It's absolutely magical.

I lean in, capturing her sexy lips with mine. Our first public kiss. She melts into me, opening her mouth to give my tongue access. Her arms wrap around me, and the act feels so much more than what it is. It's like she's announcing she's mine to the entire room. Sienna whimpers and I bite down on her bottom lip.

"If you keep making those little sounds, I'm going to gather up your dress and fuck you here for the entire room to witness." I press my forehead down on hers.

"You would allow people to see my naked pussy?"

Instead of backing down, she fucking sucks on my neck, no doubt marking me with the pressure.

"No, I'd allow them to see how pretty you look when my cock is in you." A low, rough growl leaves me and I grab her hand, leading her out of the room. If she tests me again, I will fuck her for everyone to watch.

I pull her into a room and lock the door. One side is lined with faucets and one long mirror, the other side has a couch, full-length mirror, and a half wall blocking what I'm assuming is the toilet area.

"This is the nicest bathroom I've ever been in." Sienna giggles. What it is, is a waste of space, with its rich people appointments. There are fancy single-clothed chairs to sit in. The full-length mirrors are lit from behind. Everything is made of marble and shines with luxury; even the disposable paper towel feels like cloth under my finger tips. A small white box hosts different perfumes with price tags even I would balk at, along with disposable makeup for one to take and use.

"Hands on the counter," I demand. My fingers pull at my tie and loosen it around my neck.

She eagerly does as I say and I lightly brush my hands against her naked calves and glide upwards. She turns her head to look down at me and I allow her dress to slip out of my fingers and stand.

"Eyes on the mirror and not on me."

I turn her head for her when she doesn't do it fast enough as I use my free hand to pull at my tie once again, deciding how I'm going to use the silk rope. I dangle it over her shoulders, circling her neck before I wrap it over her gorgeous eyes.

"This is what you get when you don't listen." I nip at her bottom lip and her tongue darts out to lick her swollen skin once I release her pouty flesh.

I feather my hand down her neck, over her collarbone, and between her cleavage. I watch, mesmerized by the way goosebumps follow my trail.

I take my time, pulling one thin strap down her arm, then the other, watching how her tits bare themselves for me as the straps leisurely fall down her arms.

Her chest rises and falls at a greater pace that matches her soft intake of air.

A low, appreciative growl vibrates off my lips as I take in the sight of her. "So fucking pretty."

Appreciation wells in my chest as my hands feel the curve of her hips. I love having something to grab onto. I continue on with what I was trying to do before and move her dress upwards, enjoying each part of flesh that becomes bare to me. I hike the dress up and over her ass, lacy black panties looking like a perfect semi-heart outlining her ass while the thin material disappears between her cheeks.

I kiss her soft skin, one side, then the other, worshiping her. She is my queen and she has me wanting to bow down to her.

The lace between her ass gives way easily at the tug of my fingers to give me better access. I spread her cheeks and give her one long lick. She startles at my touch, but I keep her in place with my strong hands. I don't miss how her ass wiggles after the shock of my touch.

"Such a pretty ass and pussy. Do they both want my cock?" I kiss her ass cheeks once again while my fingers slip between her legs, teasing her, I circle her inner thigh and outline her pussy lips. A smile spreads my lips up high as she wiggles, trying to place me where she wants. "You have a greedy pussy. I can feel it dripping down your leg for me."

I love the way her body responds to me, overly eager for my touch. I like drawing it out, hearing her moans and whimpers. Sounds that are solely reserved for me and no one else.

I lick her pussy from behind and she whimpers, shoving her ass into my face. *That's my girl.*

"I could survive on your taste for the rest of my life. Delicious."

My fingers spear into her and she rocks back on them as I lick her again. She encourages me with each rock, pressing her ass deeper into my face. *Fuck, yes.*

"You're so wet, your pussy is going to take my cock like the good girl you are," I murmur, in awe of how she's fucking my fingers. My words have her extending her hips further as she gets off on my dirty talk. I lick and finger fuck her, pulling out her moans that she tries to keep locked away, but it's hopeless. I continue to finger fuck her as my free hand glides up her stomach until I feel her nipple.

My fingers roll it back and forth until I can't take the pressure behind my pants anymore. Standing, I kiss her neck as the sound of my zipper joins the purr of her need for me. I watch her wiggle, wanting my touch back, as I stroke my dick twice. I line her pussy up with my cock before I plunge into her.

She moans out my name as I sink deep into her perfect velvet walls. "Sienna," I murmur, basking in the way her tight pussy clamps around my dick. I hold her tits while I thrust into her and she turns her head toward me, begging me to take her lips as I fuck her. I happily oblige. Before her, I never knew that kissing could feel so great, that it could amplify everything I feel. Before Sienna, I wasn't even a fan of the action.

My lips move from hers to her neck as I continue my assault on any piece of skin I can touch. Her pussy clamps onto my cock like a vice, her hips pummeling into me as she bounces up and down on it. It takes everything in me not to come the same time she does. I want her to milk me, take everything she needs until she's moaning my name once again. It's music to my ears.

She doesn't hold back when her orgasm hits and screams, "Oh, God! Max!" and sags against the counter.

I move her to her knees and untie the blindfold. "Open your mouth." I shove my cock in, and her mouth fucks just as good as her cunt just did. It's quickly unraveling every shred of self-control I have left.

I hiss through my teeth, trying to stay in control, but she's sucking every ounce of restraint I have out of me. I fuck her mouth, her long hair wrapped around my fist as I control both our movements. It has her sucking hard, her hands cupping my balls, and my control is lost to her. She is now the one in charge.

"This is what you do to me."

She takes me deeper, my cock hitting the back of her throat and she hums, enjoying it. It's my undoing. I come so fucking hard I see stars, and she swallows every last drop with a smile on her face.

I slowly take my cock out of her mouth and watch as her fingers push a small amount of come back between her lips.

"Thank you," she mummers, my heart twisting painfully.

I fall to my knees, matching her stance, and kiss her, allowing for all of our tastes to mix and mingle.

"You are perfect," I compliment between our lips in a hushed murmur, and I'm in complete awe of this woman who has the power to destroy me in every possible way.

Chapter 24: Sienna

♥

THE SKY IS BLUE and the temperature is perfect with no breeze to be felt. I wake up early, my feet not hurting, and with an extra pep in my step. Brute even did his morning business faster than normal; everything is going my way. It's going to be a good day. Even the air smells better than normal.

The walking sign turns just as I step up to it, not halting my perfectly-paced stroll. It's going to be a coffee and pastry type of morning. I go past the Starbucks, turning down the street to head toward the little mom-and-pop bakery that's out of my way. I think I'm going to go for the chocolate glazed croissant, one of the big ones, not those tiny two-bite types.

"Sienna!" I look toward the sound of my name, my smile never wavering. It takes me a second to place the man.

"Hi!"

It's the bartender from Oakport Beach. Now, if only I could remember his name. "What are you doing this far away from the beach?"

A relaxed chuckle leaves his lips and he looks like he can't believe his luck by running into me. "I have family here. My sister is getting married and said she would never speak to me again if I didn't close down the bar and attend."

"Families and their outrageous demands," I gasp, teasing.

I make the move to continue but he asks, "I'm heading about three stores down to get a coffee and a croissant, want to join me?"

Max is not going to like this, but it's where I'm already heading.

"You know what? You're probably rushing somewhere. It's fine." He takes a step and I spot my father down the opposite street.

"I was actually already heading there," I say, almost too quickly. "This is so rude of me, but I forgot your name."

"Elliot Eldrige." He smiles widely and extends his arm for me to follow. I step in closer than necessary, trying to hide. He places his hand on my lower back, tucking me away from sight of the other street with his bulky frame.

It's hard to keep a natural pace with the adrenaline rushing in from seeing my father. It has my muscles wanting to flee. I'm not scared of many people, but my father puts it into me.

It takes me a second to remember I'm with the bartender from Oakport Beach. He's entirely clueless that I zoned out, but he's still talking. I increase my pace, needing to get off the street, praying my father doesn't spot me. I glance behind and my father is heading in our direction but doesn't seem to have spotted me yet.

"I just can't get over what a small world this is," Elliot says, shaking his head with a smile. I wish he would stop talking and hustle his step up.

People leaving the small café hold the door open for us to walk in. To my relief, I'm able to stay hidden by Elliot's body as I step inside.

My phone buzzes and Max's name flashes over the screen. I ignore it, wanting to keep my eyes on my surroundings in case I was seen.

The crash of a ceramic coffee mug has me jumping. Shards of white porcelain scatter to the ground, the hot coffee spilling ahead of us barely missing the small child who ran into the waitress.

Elliot steps away from me to help pick up the large pieces and a worker comes around with a mop. He does it with a gracious smile. He's sweet, too sweet for my liking.

I stand there awkwardly, watching while glancing out the front windows. My phone is on a continuous buzz in my back pocket. I bring it out and find five messages from Max, but then Elliot is at my side. Together, we step in line and I order, gesturing for him to order. His wallet is out before I can hand my cash to the cashier.

"No, I asked you to come with me. This is my treat."

My phone buzzes again while Elliot pays. "Thank you."

"Am I making you late for something?" he asks while I lead us to my favorite seat in the house. It's at the back, the perfect small space to people watch everyone who strolls in for their coffee.

"What?" I ask, confused, placing my phone face down on the table.

He nods toward my device. "It hasn't stopped ringing."

I swat my hand through the air. "It's nothing."

"Boyfriend?"

I laugh at the not-so-subtle way of him fishing for information. "What if I said yes?"

"He's one lucky man."

My father walks past the window and I lean in closer to hide my face. "Thank you for thinking so." My voice comes out breathless when I wish it wouldn't, but seeing my father is making it hard to breathe.

Bram Levine is a scary-looking man. The small café stops for a second as he walks in. My heart leaps into my throat, and I'm grateful for Elliot not turning to look. I turn my head into the nook of Elliot's neck and he takes it as an advance, turning his head and pressing his lips against mine. It's soft, sweet, and does nothing for me. He doesn't even try to prod my mouth for access. He doesn't push like the nice small-town man he is.

The moment my father steps out, I turn back, my hand covering my racing heart.

"Damn girl. You know how to make a man feel wanted." He's reading my reaction all wrong. "I sure as hell hope there's no boyfriend."

"I'm sorry, I have to go." I stand, leaving my coffee on the table, untouched. I don't care how rude or bad this looks.

Sneaking a look out the door, I run the other direction toward my apartment. I take the stairs two steps at a time with my keys held between my fingers as weapons in case I need them, before I slip one into the lock and it effortlessly unlocks.

I have no time to catch my breath before handcuffs lock onto my wrists and Max is attaching them above my head.

"You've been a very bad girl, Sienna." Max could be referring to a whole lot of shit I've done.

"You need to remind me what I've been caught for." I refuse to back down or struggle.

"For allowing another man to touch you. I'm going to have to remind you that you belong to me."

"I belong to me and no one else."

"My sweet, sharp-clawed kitten, I love it when you push me." Lust fills his eyes and I struggle against his hold, even after I told myself I wouldn't. I should be furious that I'm tied up like some submissive toy, but my body excites over it. I already know this will be our goodbye to each other. After this, I'm gone. I can look out for myself better than anyone, and I'm not about to find out what will happen when I'm found and Max fails at protecting me.

"Were you jealous when you saw me kiss him?" I ask, wanting a reaction from him.

He takes his knife out, creating a small rip in my shirt between my breasts before his hands do the rest. My shirt is torn from my body and goosebumps rise at the sudden exposure to the cooler air. My breasts are held high in my push-up bra, my cleavage spilling over the top more than what's probably considered normal.

"Not as much as it dissatisfied you." His eyes sparkle with smug satisfaction. "Stop fighting who we are. We're made for each other."

I hate that he can read me so well. We both know the kiss was unmemorable at best, but if this is my punishment, I'm happy I did it.

"Stop smirking to yourself. This is a punishment. You're going to be crying for me to let you come, and only if I think you've learned your lesson will I allow you to."

Max undoes the top button of my shorts and pulls them down my legs, leaving me in my underwear. He walks around me, his gaze roaming over my bared flesh before he steps back into my line of sight and his eyes darken as he admires his view.

His knife comes up and he slips it between my breast bone and bra. I have to give the man credit, he's skilled with the knife. I plan to keep this one, just like the one I stabbed him with. My bra pops open and my heavy globes spring free, begging to be touched.

He runs his knuckles over my peaks before bringing out the nipple clamps from his pocket. "From what I remember, you like these."

"Wouldn't this be more of a punishment if you made me pleasure you?" I pant, excited to see what he plans to do with me.

"No, because we both like control, and it gets me hard watching you struggle to touch me."

He applies the clamps to both of my nipples and I watch in awe as he kneels before me. He's so handsome with a few stray hairs falling over his forehead and into his right eye. His hair is longer than when we first met, like he hasn't had time to cut it.

The movement has his leather and metal scent circling around me. He places a soft kiss to my leg, his hands roaming up my skin until he squeezes my ass with both hands. His face is right at my pussy, my panties the only thing between us. Inch by inch, he pulls my panties down, pausing when I'm bared to him. My heart plunges and flip flops all around with the way Max is staring at me. Our connection feels raw, too heavy for what we are, and I have to glance away.

"You're already dripping for me and I've hardly touched you yet."

My hands move, begging to run my fingers through his hair and help control his movements. He glances up, winking, before my panties are brought down to my feet and he commands, "Step." I walk out of them without further prompting.

He brings them to his nose, inhaling deeply. "Sweetest pussy I've ever had." I watch in disbelief as he places them into his back pocket. "I'm going to jerk off with these tonight to the memory of you."

I roll my eyes, but his words send a flutter of excitement through me. We regard each other for a beat, the moment adding to the crackle of electricity in the air. Max looks so playful when he's relaxed and feeling comfortable.

Taking his sweet ass time, he inserts one finger into me, but it's not enough. My hips move to help, wanting more. He slips two, then three fingers in, and my head falls back with a moan. His fingers move harder, my body keeping up with his rhythm, even with my legs shaking.

His mouth latches onto my clit and he licks, sucks, nibbles, working me into a frenzy.

"Max," I moan. I'm so damn close.

Then he pulls away. I'm panting, my body still moving to his rhythm, like I can imagine him still there.

"Max, what the fuck?" I holler, frustrated and annoyed that my orgasm is at the brink of making me come apart.

"You better make me come or fuck me right this instant." I'm delirious. I could feel it was going to be an epic one, you know the type that makes your entire being levitate and lasts forever? This was going to be one of those.

He pulls out a small gun-like contraption, his thumb continuing to brush against my skin like he can't stop touching me.

"Let me tattoo you." It's not a demand, but it's not a question, either.

"What the fuck? Finish one job before you move on to the next." My voice is needy as hell and my arms pull against the cuffs, wanting to finish the job myself.

"Fuck no," I pout, still struggling, but it's not because I don't trust him. Max stands and the bulge in his pants is clear as day. He's getting off on this, just like he said he would.

"Then you don't come, simple as that."

I growl, irritated. "How do you want to mark me?"

"Property of Max."

My chest wants to cave in on itself. The thought is sweet and very permanent. Nothing in my life has ever been everlasting. What this is, can't be forever. I don't understand how Max can't see it.

"Are you fucking crazy?"

"Actually, yes. I had a psych evaluation once, and they said so, but I think my mother also paid them to say that. I guess none of us will ever really know." He shrugs with one shoulder, turning on the machine in his fingertips.

He's not meeting my eyes and I stop fighting my restraints. "Look at me, Max." He fiddles, getting the tattoo gun ready, and I speak again, "Max." He brings his gaze to me, vulnerability shining in his eyes clear as day. "I love you, so I must be crazy too."

Shock resonates through him, evident in the way he flinches and his eyes clear with an emotion I can't pinpoint.

"Tattoo me, Max." I say softly, and this time I have no reservations. "Somewhere discreet."

A smile tugs at his lips, each second it stretches his face wider. He stands, pulling my face to his, and kisses me. It's rough, dominating and demanding. It's everything a goodbye kiss should be.

He moves around me and I can feel his energy and warmth from behind before his hand feathers over my ass cheek. The first pressure of the gun has me jumping. "Stay still, my love."

"What does it say?" I ask once he's cleaned and bandaged it.

"His only." He comes around to my front. "Mine says, 'Her only'." He lifts up his pant leg and there is beautiful lettering on his calf. "I love you too, Sienna." He kisses me again, but this one is soft, gentle, as he takes his time exploring my mouth.

His mouth refuses to leave mine, kissing me like I'm his lifeline. My once-forgotten nipple clamps are released, the sensation of relief, pain, and pleasure zips over me, causing me to moan.

This man can kiss. The sound of his zipper echoes around us before his hands land on my ass and I'm lifted up. I'm brought down onto his cock, my legs wrapping around his hips as he fucks me.

My body thrums with Max touching me. He brings a sense of comfort that I've never had with anyone before. His lips release mine, and he's wearing a soft expression, his eyes dark and shining. He makes a show of latching onto my nipple and sucking, knowing he has my complete and utter attention. It is the sexiest thing I've ever seen.

My orgasm builds once again as his cock thickens inside me, stretching me further. I come hard before he places me back on my feet and his come streams onto my stomach and pussy. His hands smear it in. "You look gorgeous covered in my come."

He's back kissing me again, pulling my body in close, not caring if he gets some of his semen on himself.

"I can't share you anymore, Sienna. I'm done competing with Dante. You're not to go back to Throne of Sin."

I don't register his words at first. He unlocks me, my wrists bursting with pins and needles with the extra blood flow when they come down.

"What?" I ask, confused.

"It's driving me too crazy. I'm slipping when I shouldn't be."

My spine straightens, wanting to fight him on this, but what's the point? I plan on leaving anyway. Why waste our last moments fighting?

"Fine," I concede.

"Sienna, you're mine and not going back there." He's so damn handsome when he gets riled up and all possessive. "Wait, what?"

His eyes narrow, not expecting me to give in so easily.

"Max, I just let you tattoo my ass and give me a mind-blowing orgasm. Let's just enjoy our time right now. Maybe when I come back to my senses, I'll fight you on it, but for now, let's enjoy our time."

"Damn right, you're going to listen to me like a good girl," he teases, still watching me with caution like I'm going to change my mind any moment.

"Lay down with me." I crawl onto the bed, lying on my untattooed side. He's still watching me with hesitation. "If you don't take your spot, I'll call Brute over and he will."

Max shakes his head but crawls onto the bed and holds me in his arms.

Chapter 25: Max

♥

I'M GOING OVER THE family's bank accounts trying to figure out how someone has stolen a half million dollars without anyone batting an eye. Every account is the same. Small amounts that fly under the radar.

I go to the surveillance I placed on Sienna, but she doesn't open those bank accounts. I dig deeper, trying to find where this money has been transferred. I stare at the name for a half hour, not believing it. Sienna Levine.

My blood runs cold. Sienna loves my brother like family. She loves *me*. How could we all be so blind to this? An iciness drips into me, refreezing my thawing heart. I don't want to believe it.

There has to be a glitch or a reason for it. My fingers strum on the desk before I shut everything off. I know better than to jump into the deep end and assume the worst, because if it is true, my family will murder her. It won't matter what I say or do. I can't protect her from this and I'd never be able to forgive my family.

My hand pulls at the skin of my face and I blow out a breath. My mind is a gigantic raging beast that's clearly not thinking straight. I could hide this for her and tell Romeo and Dante I came up empty. All rational thoughts have flown the coop. I could kill them before they get to her. The only thing my future holds is red of some sort. Red from her blood, from my family's blood, or from mine. It doesn't matter. Everything has changed in the blink of an eye.

Just like the past. Fear of the unknown pushes the hairs up along my arms. The smell of the pig farm Romeo and I had to endure fills my nostrils, although there's no rational reason for this to happen. Memories of having to butcher and dispose of so many come to the forefront of my mind.

I used to see their faces when I slept, when I woke, until one day I made the conscious decision to not give a fuck anymore. I went hunting on my own soon after that. The faces disappeared, I lost my humanity, as my brother used to say.

He always teased me that a woman would bring it back, but I don't think anyone could've foreseen her also being the one to take it away again. If these feelings are what I'm missing, I want none of it. It was easier before, when I wasn't contemplating killing my family, or the woman I love, because I won't survive it if either of those jobs are passed down to me.

Don't get ahead of yourself...

She may have a logical explanation. I'm heading toward her apartment before I realize I'm halfway there.

The vibration from hitting her door over and over again rattles up and down my forearm before I open the door myself. Her suitcase is at the door and she's standing there, shell-shocked by my intrusion. Brute wags his tail, happy to see me, but Sienna's face shows none of that happiness. Her hair has been changed to a deep scarlet red that matches blood when it first hits oxygen.

I storm in, my adrenaline leading the way, and I see a fucking piece of paper on the table with my name. My eyes scan the micro room and see all of Brute's shit in one pile. My eyes glance back to the paper and I pick it up while keeping Sienna in my sight at all times. She stands there, not moving. Good fucking thing because I like when she's tied up and at my mercy.

"You're asking me to take care of your fucking dog?" I look up toward my cameras. They're intact, working. How did I miss this?

"I overrode them to make sure you saw what I wanted you to." Her voice is so fucking small, laced with guilt that my heart still refuses to accept.

"What if I didn't come by? You would do this to a poor, innocent animal? You chose him. You picked him, and now he's useless to you so you just leave?" I'm not sure if I'm actually talking about her dumb dog that I love or about myself. Someone who she *should* love.

"You come by every night. You two have a bond I never had with him."

"Dogs can sense when you don't like them." I scoff. "Dogs are fucking smart." I give my head a good shake, hoping to knock some sense into myself.

"Why?" I ask. "I could have given you everything. I would have moved mountains if that's what it took." I rip up her shitty letter that asks me to take her dog in. It says nothing about forgiveness. Nothing about loving me. I'm not even a thought in her mind, unlike how she is in mine. I was prepared to murder my bloodline to keep her safe. I would have given my own life if it meant she was happy. I'd die a happy man knowing she would continue to smile.

"I loved you." My voice cracks like a pussy. "You're like a sister to my brother. We trusted you."

She stills, her spine growing rigid.

"Did you do it?" I ask, praying she has no idea what I'm talking about. I didn't want to ask, the full, clear sentence unwilling to go past my tongue.

"I did what I had to do. It's nothing personal. No one missed it." She's emotionless, uncaring in the way she talks. What the fuck? It's like this is no big deal, and her tone is almost as if telling me to get over it. "Anyway, I just returned it all not even five minutes ago. Go check. It's all fucking there."

Betrayal.

The thought of it gets lodged in my throat. It's thick and suffocating. No matter how hard I try to swallow it down, it stays at my Adam's apple, unmoving.

"It's not about the money," I whisper, my vocal cords unable to produce any more volume. "We trusted you."

"You should have killed me when you had the chance." Defiance is dark in her irises as she glares at me.

"You can't possibly mean that."

"My father killed my mother for betrayal. It's in my blood."

I can't believe the things coming out of her mouth. I thought I knew her. My heart squeezes like a vice has been clamped on to it. It's being pulled and it hurts so fucking much. I've forgotten what the sensation of pain feels like and understand why I turned it off.

I pull up my phone and send a quick pin drop. My finger catches one lone tear that she's forcing out to make me feel more. I won't have any of it. Fake tears do nothing for me.

"It's time I correct my first mistake." My voice drops and becomes hauntingly dark. I haven't heard this tone from myself since my father was alive. The blood in my veins hums with a destructive energy that has me shaking and wishing for bloodshed.

"You couldn't have possibly loved me, Max," she has the audacity to say, telling me my own truth.

"We will never know now." I turn back around, my hand gripping the wooden door. "And take care of your own fucking dog." I slam the door, its hinges rocking in their sockets. That bloodthirst I have tried to repress is clawing under my skin. The monster in me wants its freedom, but I keep walking. If I turn around, I can't trust what I would do.

The glass door at the entrance cracks as I slam my fist against it. Her father sits right where I left my pin drop.

"I've just texted you her apartment number," I spit on my way out, Sienna's father's hand catching the door.

Sienna

WHAT I DIDN'T EXPECT to see was the hurt I caused in Max's face. The other thing...him letting me go. Maybe I was banking on being forced to stay and have him keep me in this weird, twisted world we live in. But he just left. Let me go like I wasn't worth his time. I was expecting a fight, a blowout, *something*, anything more than what happened.

I pull out the second letter I wrote him, the one telling him that I do love him and explaining about the money. I knew they would find it soon enough, and I wanted a chance to explain my side and the reason I returned it all.

I suppose there's no point in leaving it here now. My hands rip it in half and continue until it's just bigger than the size of a quarter and leave the shreds scattered on the table.

My door pounds three times. *Max. He came back.* My shoulders sag with relief as I open the door, preparing myself for the real fight this time.

"Officer?" I look past him before my eyes land on his badge. "McCain. What are you doing in these parts?"

"What a small world it is, Sienna. Sorry to be pounding on your door like this. I was called in for a break in a few doors over and wanted to see if any of the neighbors had seen anything."

The top of my father's head bobs as he climbs up the stairs toward my floor. I open my door up wider. "Come on in."

Clayton steps in, noting my suitcase. "Going somewhere?" he asks.

My hand rubs at the back of my neck. "I'm a bit of a nomad and travel where my heart leads me."

"It would be just my luck, I leave Oakport Beach to see you here but you're leaving."

He's giving me a shy, boyish look. It's adorable. If only good boys were my thing.

Chapter 26: Max

♥

R OMEO'S NUMBER SLIDES ACROSS my phone for the second time before my fingers swipe to ignore. I need a second to collect my thoughts. Sienna was leaving me a fucking Dear John letter. It's as bad as the admiration letter I got this morning. I have to give whoever is sending me those letters credit; I can't find them, and I can find *anyone*. Deep down I know I haven't put that much time into it. I've been too consumed with Sienna.

That's ending now. I'm getting my old self back. I've righted the world by giving her back to her father. It will be as if I never entered into her world. I've wiped the slate clean of our meeting. Everything will go back to its natural order. It has to.

My silent alarm goes off for Throne of Sin. Of course, this would be the day my world explodes and doesn't give me a minute to myself.

I call my brother back and he starts speaking the moment it connects. "We need you at Throne of Sin; it's being raided by the cops."

I jump on my motorcycle, going into protection mode. It's easier to flip my switch than to think about what just happened. Dante better have gotten his ass out of there before they showed up.

By the time I'm there, all the girls are in the backs of cop cars.

"What's the meaning of this?" I ask, pushing my way through the swarm of cops to get closer to the front door.

"Are you Dante Mancini?" The cop is looking down his nose at me, like I'm the scum of the world. I'm not dressed in a nice suit like my brother always wears. I'm wearing dirty jeans and a tight black T-shirt under my leather jacket. I flick up my aviators to look him in the eye. It would take me one week of planning and his family would never see him again.

"Yeah, I'm him," I lie, tilting my chin up and throwing him my best tough-guy attitude.

Cold cuffs are immediately snapped onto my wrists. I don't bother fighting them. This will give Dante more time to get the fuck out of whatever this is. I don't fight the arrest, only half listening. It sounds like human trafficking bullshit.

My rights are read to me as I'm pulled toward a cop car and my head is pushed down. I'm not worried. Dante will make the necessary calls and, by the time we get to the station, I'll be free to walk.

Shelby gives me a little wave and I note her hands aren't handcuffed. A few of the girls are crying, scared that Dante can't protect them.

Not once has this place been targeted before. We have half the police force on our salary. I memorize every law enforcement face; they will not go unpunished. I suppose this is a shit place for me, the family lawyer, to be sitting. There's no doubt Romeo will have to call his sister-in-law, Aria Rossi, to help us out of this one. Ironic thing is, she was once the sinful daughter for falling in love with a cop.

Two cops get in the front, not bothering to look back at me. "You know my name. Wouldn't it be fair if I knew yours?"

They ignore me, and that's when I spot the bartender from that small-ass beach town. He's standing off to the side, watching all of this go down and looking perplexed that Throne of Sin is now closed. Strange.

We stop at the back of the station and I'm led inside like a dog on a chain. I fucking hate it.

They put me into a small room then cuff me to the chair and the table. The whole game of power is unimpressive, too showboaty for my personal taste. There's a camera set up in the corner, directed at me. No other cameras that I can see, and no two-way mirrors.

My head jerks back when I see Clayton McCain walk in and close the door. Shock flows through me seeing the useless beach cop in the city. Why the fuck is he here? He walks toward the camera, turning it on, the red lights shining to life.

"Dante is going to have a few human trafficking charges laid against him." He whistles, folding up a few pieces of paper on a clipboard. "It's an impressive list."

My lips purse and my jaw clenches, but other than that I don't move a muscle. My body stays looking relaxed in my chair when I'm anything but.

"Too bad you're his brother, Maximus Mancini, and this has nothing to do with you."

I cock a brow. "Did you just figure that out now, or did you know the moment they arrested me?"

He smiles at me like we're two friends catching up. This entire room makes my skin crawl, it feels smaller than it is.

"Me? I did nothing. You're the one who took his place, just like I knew you would." He takes a seat across from me, leaning over to press a button on the camera. "I'm impressed how fast you came. You had me second guessing myself."

"What's with the camera?"

"Oh, that." He swipes his hand like it's insignificant. "I'm videoing us, and later I will place sound over it. It's amazing what AI technology can do now. I can have you saying anything I want."

I know this game. "What do you want?"

"I can make all of these charges go away for Dante. It will be like it never happened."

There it is.

"And what do I have to do?" I suck on my canine tooth, annoyed, while assessing McCain.

"I have to say this is a little surreal for me. You sitting in cuffs and me talking to you."

"What do you want?" I ask again, my patience gone.

"I have one question. What made Sienna different?"

I can't hide the shock that must resonate on my face. My eyes grow large before I can attempt to school my features. Now I'm taking a second look at this officer. His breathing is normal, a cocky smirk on his lips. He thinks he has me.

"What does this have to do with her?"

"Funny story. I think she thought you were coming back to knock on her door but she found me instead."

My jaw clenches, every muscle involuntarily contracting. Rage simmers deep within my bones. I haven't felt this type of reaction since I was a teenager.

"This is how it's going to go…" He pauses for what I think is effect. I want to rip my cuffs off and go wolverine on him. "She's fine. I'm keeping with your plan of sending her back to her father. Honestly, I think that's the best idea you've had since you met her. I just wanted to talk to her to see what all the fuss was about."

I can't help myself and my hands pull at the cuffs, making the metal-on-metal ting and my wrists burn from the harsh pull.

"I have another fun fact that I think you'll be interested in. I have it on good authority that this station is about to find the graveyard of your trophies."

I scoff, "I burn my victims." My mouth snaps closed as I realize what I just said.

Clayton covers his mouth and leans in. "That's the thing, you don't anymore. I've been a busy boy. I thought by now you would have wanted to meet me. I'm almost more famous than you, but I suppose they don't know about me."

My mouth dries. All the articles that Romeo kept showing me that I blew off. "You're too unoriginal to do your own work, huh?"

"I like to call it smart, but tomayto, tomahto." His head bounces right to left with each word.

"You'll never get away with it. Our differences will be noticed."

He leans back and chuckles. "This isn't my first rodeo. I'm a fucking hero when it comes to serial killers. That's why I was asked to come up here and leave my post. Every now and then different districts search me out and I find what no one else can." He makes a kissing motion with his fingers in front of his mouth.

"She's yours then." I shrug. "I already said my goodbye to her." My heart constricts as I say the words, but my face stays stoic.

"It's killing you inside, isn't it?" He wants a reaction from me, but he won't get one.

"I thought you've done your homework. She betrayed my family and the entertainment value of her is gone now. You should know I have a short attention span when it comes to the pets I acquire."

"I was thinking that too." He waves his finger around. "But then I started to really take note. You love her. She's different."

I give him what I think is an unimpressed bored face. Sienna was never meant to be more than a plaything I enjoyed. She and I have run our course. Deep down, I knew she wouldn't live long anyway. This guy is doing me a favor. He's making himself the bad guy and not me or my family.

"I'd shake your hand if I could." I nod toward my shackles. "I'd say you have everything under control. Just let me know when I can be on my merry way. Maybe tell me where the graveyard is as a professional courtesy, that way I won't mess up what you clearly worked so hard to do."

He sighs like this conversation pains him. "It's not that easy anymore. You see, I don't have the authority to let you go. The big wig here will have to take a look at the video, but he's not going to like what he hears. You've just confessed to being the area's most notorious serial killer. You're making a lot of people's careers in the next day or two."

He gives me some weird ass look that I think is his evil grin. "But maybe I could help you out..."

I bite my inner cheek, hating this man and the corner he has me backed into.

"Did you know I wanted to ask Sienna out for coffee? But every time I tried you were already there." He shakes his head in disbelief. "I have no luck with women. My fiancé left me at the altar the day before my wedding. Maybe you could kill her for me."

I have no interest in doing this man's dirty work. "Why can't you?"

His eyes grow large and he bobs his head again. "Small town. I'd be the first suspect. It's always the people closest to you."

"Sure." I plan to kill him, not the poor girl. He assesses me but seems content with my lie.

"Good. I'm sure your family will be able to get you out of here in no time. Good luck." McCain strides out of the room and all I can imagine is killing him.

Chapter 27: Sienna

♥

BRUTE LICKS MY FACE while I'm tied up in my own bed, pondering the fact that I'm surrounded by crazy people all the time. It never ends. I lie here, bored because I know Max will come for me. He has to.

My arms are numb by the time I finally hear the door to my apartment open and close. I should be more frightened. Rationally, I keep telling myself this, and can't understand why I'm not freaking out more.

Officer McCain makes his appearance by leaning over top of my head when I don't bother to look up.

"You're a popular girl, Sienna." He unlatches my hands and I immediately rub at them, trying to get some blood flow back. He continues, undoing my feet and humming as he goes about it. "Sorry for tying you up, I couldn't trust you would be here by the time I made it back."

What the fuck?

I stand and rush to use the bathroom, slamming the door behind me. "Take your time," he says from the other side of the door.

The vent overhead has the air conditioner nipping at the back of my neck. My eyes frantically look for an escape route. There isn't a window in here to escape from. I'm stuck having to go back out that door. Finishing up, I wash my hands and walk out, curious what's in store for me next.

McCain isn't standing guard by the bathroom door like I expected. Hesitantly, I enter the main room and stop mid step when I see my father standing there. "I thought it was only fair since this is what Max wanted. I felt it was unfair to keep you."

My mouth gapes open before I can close it. The MC has and always will come first for this man; before family, before everything, no matter what. I'm well aware that I've made myself club business.

"Daughter."

"Prez." My father narrows his eyes at my greeting.

I had always toed the line and done what has been asked of me. I had striven to gain his attention, wanting him to be proud of me. It has taken me this long to realize I was always just a pawn on his leash, until I broke free.

"It's time to get you married." His hard eyes hold my gaze, waiting for me to submit like I always do and give him what he wants.

"Who's the new guy in line to take Vice Prez?" I shouldn't be poking the bear but I can't help it. McCain snickers, grabbing a handful of the popcorn that sits in a bowl on the table.

My father's jaw locks and it takes a moment for him to unhinge it to speak. The first signs of dread flicker over me and I swallow. A small smile overtakes his lips, his jaw finally unclenching. "I think I misspoke. You are already married. It's time to make it official."

It's like a cold bucket of water being poured over my head.

"Your husband is alive and well. It took a few weeks in the hospital to recover, but he's as good as new."

Dread knots in my throat, making it hard to breathe.

"Oh, you thought he was dead?" My father's tone is menacing, mocking.

"I can't wait to see how this plays out." I forgot about McCain being here and glance over my shoulder. He shoves another handful of popcorn into his mouth and his words are muffled as he speaks. "I love a good family reunion."

My father grips my shoulder and pulls me forward.

"Just one second," Clayton says from behind. His front touches my back and he leans in for only me to hear. "Don't worry, I won't let them kill you. I have another plan in mind."

Chapter 28: Max

♥

"**M**AXIMUS MANCINI."

I've been held for almost twenty-four hours by the time my name is called. I suppose they now know I'm not my brother. My skin crawls with the idea of Officer McCain. He has to be the one who sent me those letters.

Every fiber in my body is screaming for me to kill him. I hate the idea of him out in the world and not knowing what he has planned. His plan, obviously, is not to watch me rot in prison. Surely, he wouldn't let me out just to kill an old girlfriend.

I walk out of the interrogation room and make my way to the front desk where my few personal items are handed back to me. I refuse to growl a thank you. Romeo's sister-in-law, Aria, is standing out front waiting. Neither of us say anything until we're sitting in the back of her car and the car is on the road.

"How did you get me out?" My eyes narrow in on hers. I trust no one. Maybe she's working with McCain.

"Last I checked, you weren't Dante," she says matter-of-factly. "Don't worry, he's not being pulled in. They were fishing, that's all."

"Thank you for coming," I grumble, on edge.

Aria isn't taking any of my bullshit and glares at me like an ungrateful child. "Gia is quite fond of you," she refers to her sister, Romeo's wife. "And Romeo refused to take no for an answer," she tells me, her stern voice barely softened by a sarcastic chuckle. Then she replaces her bad attitude with a warm smile.

"You don't like being strong-armed into doing dirty work for us, do you?" My lips twist with my immature blow, but she stays unfazed.

"I've heard you're the asshole brother. I didn't do it for you." She waves her hand. "All your brothers are on their way to Throne of Sin to meet with you."

I turn, looking out the window, my thoughts swirling with what needs to be done.

I step through Throne of Sin's doors a few minutes later and Dante whistles me over with a head nod as he continues toward his office. He's not happy to see me, his expression says it all. I'm sure he thinks all of his problems with this place are because of me.

Ignoring the scowling face of Dante, I head toward the bar and pour myself a whiskey, not waiting for the new bartender to do their job.

Each step he takes toward me is stiff. He might need a drink more than I do. I pour two more shots, holding one out for him.

"You're not going to like this, but it can't be avoided," I say as he downs the drink.

The vein in his forehead protrudes along with his angry, bulging eyes. Life is so much easier when you don't let shit bother you. Cutting ties to your emotions frees the soul.

"And the blows keep coming," he mumbles, pushing off the counter, heading toward his office. "What's the issue now?" he asks, his back to me.

"She's not coming back." The words are hard to push out and come out lower than intended, and the first pit of pain wants to burrow in but I refuse to allow it.

"How and why would you know Sienna is not coming back?" We enter the office and he taps his fist on the arm chair, looking down at it, lost in thought, before he glances back at me.

My first instinct is to say she's mine, but I let her go. "I'm the one who told her to come here to work, because I knew her family would never dare to look for her here."

I continue telling him the whole story of how it came to be. Dante is furious with my intrusion into his business. I've already stopped the other brothers from coming here, he's too wound up to see reason right now.

·❤·❤·❤·❤·❤·

I WANT TO TEXT Sienna and my fingers itch to glide over the screen. I have to toss my phone across the room and pull out a textbook to distract myself. The letters and numbers get jumbled somewhere between the page and my head. It's impossible to concentrate. *This is a first.* It always helped before, but now it's like my brain can only focus on one thing: Sienna.

Maybe she's still at her apartment? No, she's back home where she belongs. I should have continued on with my task instead of becoming distracted with her. If I had, would Sienna's future have been better than what it has become?

I drop my head into my palm, my elbow resting on the table.

One look, that's all I need.

I stand, leaving the table a mess. My hand touches the door handle at the same time as my phone rings. It could be her...more importantly, it could be my brother.

Pressing the phone to my ear, Romeo begins, "I have something to show you, meet me at the butcher shop." He hangs up before I can get a word in.

I'm torn between the two, but in the end, he can wait.

THE CLUBHOUSE IS AS busy as I've ever seen it. I walk in with no one noticing except one scrawny teenager. "Exciting night," I say, nodding my head toward his empty vest with no patches.

"I'm getting patched in." The boy is giddy, practically jumping up and down. All he will be is this clubs bitch until someone says he's worthy. I want to tell him to find worth in himself but that's not how these people roll.

Looking around, I realize a new club is joining them.

My eyes pause when they land on Sienna sitting next to her *husband*. I have to step closer to make sure. I killed the fucker, hadn't I? I try thinking back to that night and I can't remember if I checked for a pulse. It normally doesn't matter because I burn everyone, but I left him as a warning to those who dare to touch what's mine.

My heart stills seeing Sienna with a fake smile plastered on her face. This is all I wanted. I got my look, I can go, but my feet refuse to listen to reason. They stay firmly in place. It takes an hour before my muscles allow me to tear them away from this place.

"WHERE HAVE YOU BEEN?" Romeo tosses a paper in front of me. "Listen, I know you're going through something right now, but you have to stop."

"Stop what?"

"The butchering. Damn it, Maximus. I thought you were trying to slow down."

I scratch at my ear, the smell of fresh meat from the store wafting all around me. "I don't know what you're talking about."

My brother levels me with the same look our father used to give us, his eyes going from me to the paper. I pick it up and read the headlines.

My jaw locks, my molars grinding against each other. "This isn't me," I spit out, annoyed that my brother would even question me.

"It has all of your call signs," he bites, frustration coloring his face.

"From twenty years ago. I burn everyone now."

He scoffs, giving me an exaggerated pointed glare. "No, you burn the ones you don't want anyone to find. This is still what you do when you are cocky enough to leave a message."

"It's a copycat. The cop held me for twenty-four hours and he knew I wasn't Dante."

"You're getting out of control. Dante said you've grown obsessed with his bartender, Sienna." *Out of control?* The condescension rolling off my brother's gaze tells me he thinks *I'm* the problem. To piss him off as much as he's infuriating me, I lean back, giving him a nice, sweet smile.

"He's just pissed that she left and he had to go get a new bartender."

"Max, don't you see how sloppy you have become? Leave that poor girl alone."

"Sienna is mine," I growl, baring my teeth like a rabid dog. A knot forms in my throat, braiding its way down until it twists at my heart.

"But are you hers, Max?" He waits a few beats. The silence causes me to breathe harder. "Keep this crazy up and we're going to have the cops sniffing around. We can't afford the heat right now." Our father's voice comes out of him and it's like I'm twelve years old again.

I walk out, my shoulder hitting the doorway. My head spins, my breathing forced yet little comes in and out. My hand slams into the entrance door, its glass cracking at the force before I'm out in the fresh air. The butcher smell is lodged in my nose, refusing to let me breathe anything else in.

"You're a worthless heir. You can't even help feed your family. This meat is worthless. I can't sell it. We can't eat it."

My father grabs the back of my neck, drawing me to the saw we used to butcher the meat. My face is an inch away and he still pushes harder. I close my eyes, feeling my head go closer, the wind from the table on my forehead. I draw in a breath, unwilling to breathe or move until the force is gone. I almost fall into the saw at the absence of his grip, but my hands catch me and I fall down to the floor.

"You're pathetic, boy, a waste of an heir."

My hand touches my eyebrow and red coats my fingertips.

I push the memory out, trying to remember the last equation I was working on.

Slowly, I'm able to breathe properly.

Chapter 29: Sienna

♥

SINCE BEING ESCORTED BACK to my father's club, I've been banished to my new room. Someone stands guard at my door at all times and I've hardly seen my husband. *Something is off.*

My door opens and a guard walks in. "Your husband has requested your presence."

I walk toward the room I've been summoned to. It's the shitty conference room where they hold church.

"We're throwing a party tonight," my father tells me once I'm seated. Jack beams at me with a creepy smile.

"Nothing changes," I mutter loud enough for both of them to hear. Neither of their expressions falter. Before Max, before the wedding, my father would have frowned, lecturing me about not misbehaving.

"You will wear the dress I choose for you, Wife," Jack replies, his eyes looking me up and down. They don't flash or look impressed the way Max's always did.

My stomach twists, thinking about my last words to him. I was scared, not knowing how to deal with it.

"What's the occasion?"

"You," my father answers.

Jack adds, "It's the wedding celebration we never had, and we plan to announce us going legit."

"I thought the one percenter patch was a badge of honor," I repeat the words my father preached my entire childhood.

They both chuckle. "Oh, we are still going to be one percenters, but we're helping to clear our name for outsiders. We just need to make the impression we're trying to clean up our name."

"Can I go now?" I don't care what their plan is, I'll keep playing their game until I can slip away. The next time I leave, no one will find me.

I EXPECTED A STRIPPER dress to be sent to my room, and you can imagine my surprise when a cute, sporty tennis dress shows up for me. It fits like a glove. The shorts underneath have a pocket that fits my phone and any weapon I'd like to conceal, like the nice knife I stole from Max.

The dress may seem dull and boring to some, but this will place me as the most dressed-up person at the party.

An hour later, I'm dragged down to the party by my elbow and instructed to sit on the bar. I'm on display for the club to see my loyalty.

No one stops and stares at Jack like he should be dead. Thinking back to that night, the room was so red, how could he have survived?

I focus my attention on the new prospects forced to wait on everyone. They're shitty at their job. It takes everything in me not to jump behind the counter and take over the bartending. The tips would be nice, since I no longer have an account with money in it.

Goosebumps rise along my arms and up my neck and that familiar feeling I get when Max is around trickles over me. My eyes search the dark corners of the room. He has to be here, even though I can't see him. Flutters ignite in my stomach and I'm about to jump down when Jack appears out of nowhere, placing his hand on my thigh. My face falls as I move my leg out of his grasp.

"Careful, Wife, we don't want to start the celebration too early." His tone has my blood turning to ice and a pit grows in my stomach.

"By the looks of it, you were celebrating a moment ago," I sass, narrowing my eyes.

"I was under the impression you didn't want to warm my bed." My heart beats wildly at the thought of having to do that. I look past Jack and he steps to the side, blocking my view once again. Jack's chin drops, assessing me. "That's what I thought."

That's when I see him. Max is standing to the side, his eyes trained on me, his arms crossed over his chest. My muscles tense seeing him and Jack pinches at my shoulder. "Relax, this is going to be one hell of a party tonight."

My hands itch to push myself off the counter, but I stay sitting with my back perfectly straight. Jack laughs, shaking his head and walking away from me, unaware of Max's presence. I try not to stare at Max, he's clearly trying not to draw attention to himself, even though he does nothing to mask his presence. It's like no one sees him. I suppose it must be very similar to the day he came to kill my father, but saw me instead.

Max takes a step and my eyes grow wide as I watch him walk toward me like he owns the room. I glance around, looking to see if my father is watching. He's about two feet from Max in deep conversation. Jack is on the deck having a smoke. Max keeps his strides steady as he comes closer.

I jump down from the counter, my runners not making a sound on the floor. The smell of marijuana filters toward me from somewhere nearby. We're only about five feet away from each other.

My heart is pumping at an alarming rate. I didn't expect I would see him again. He's more handsome than what my memory held for me. He's wearing faded jeans that fit him perfectly, reminding me how strong and powerful he is. Even though his T-shirt looks as old as him, it stretches in all the right places, highlighting every muscle he has. The people step out of his way, he is unaware of the dominance he holds over everyone. It's subconscious, it makes him lethal. Everything is tempting about him, no wonder I was drawn to him in the first place.

I should have realized that Max would always land back in my life. He's lured in by the chaos of my life.

Blocking my view, Elliot, the Oakport Beach bartender, comes into my vision. "Sienna. You're a hard girl to track down."

My head flinches back slightly, not expecting to see him. "Umm...hi?" My head tilts with confusion. This doesn't look to be his scene. "What are you doing here?"

He runs his hand through his hair. It's then I notice everyone is staring at this guy in a suit. He sticks out like a sore thumb among the riffraff of this MC.

"I wanted to ask you out to coffee again." He shrugs, giving me a shy, crooked smile.

I can't believe this poor guy came here to ask me out. *How the heck did he even find me?* I glance up to find Jack coming back in from having a smoke.

"This is not the place or time," I hiss, my lips flat with worry of what my husband or father will do if they see this guy. The volume in the room drops an octave but maintains its background noise. Everyone is listening to our conversation.

Max is closer, watching our exchange, and I can't tell what he's thinking.

Elliot extends his hand. "Walk with me," he pleads, his eyes so damn sincere.

My feet refuse to move as I watch the room around us, worried that this could be the spark that lights everything up.

Max

SIENNA LOOKS STUNNING IN her little white sporty dress thing. Her ass is begging to be handled by my palm. My eyes are only on her as I take each step until the small-town bartender decides he has a death wish.

The air in the room changes, the energy vibrating with anxious anticipation. I pause, not interfering, wanting to see how this goes.

Sienna's fake smile is gone, replaced with a gentle frown as she tries to let this guy off the hook too nicely. It's rather convenient he's here and not in Oakport Beach.

I press my tongue to the top of my mouth to stop me from saying something that will draw attention to me. By nightfall, Sienna will be mine once again.

My eyes fly to the front when red and blue lights scatter across the dim house. It's like the whole room goes into slow motion as I watch everything play out. Jack and her father cheers their cans of beer, each aluminum can denting. They watch as mayhem ignites their club. *What am I missing?*

Elliot begs Sienna to take his hand while everyone else is frantic, running in every direction, trying to escape the cops. My back straightens. Jack, Bram, and even possibly Elliot expected the cops. They're the only fuckers not stressing out.

The pretty boy is trying to grab her hand but Sienna just stands there, shooing him, trying to get him to leave. I step up, my side touching hers now. "She said leave."

He opens and closes his mouth before running with no direction in mind like everyone else.

The place still smells of weed and cigarettes as the officers walk into an almost-vacant clubhouse. There are still a few random people freaking out, hiding in odd places.

"What can we help you with?" her father asks the officers.

The police hardly glance at the two men and walk right over to us. "Sienna Levine?" they question.

"Yes?" Her voice is uncertain, her eyes darting to her father, me, and the cops.

"You are under arrest..." They handcuff her, reading her rights. It's not until now that I realize what I fear, and that's losing her.

Chapter 30: Max

♥

I'M FROZEN AS I watch Sienna being arrested for the attempted murder of Jack Pierce. It should be me. Instead, it's her being punished for my crime.

My sin.

My fuck up.

Suddenly, I'm that scared little boy who's standing outside his home staring at his dead father's head, yet in my mind, his lips are still moving, yelling at me for being a fuck up. For not being able to concentrate hard enough to earn the right to be his heir. He even told me he was happy I wasn't second in line and that Romeo was when our oldest brother died.

Like the fuck up I am, I stand there, my feet unmoving. I swear, not even my eyes are blinking as I watch my girl being handcuffed. Her eyes lock on to mine, a single tear escaping over her lashes. Her face is so beautiful, even when she's dejected. She refuses to allow another salty drop to escape.

The cop hauls her away with unnecessary force, her feet tripping from the sudden movement. I'm forced to witness her suffering for my crime, my attempted murder.

Her head hangs down, but I'm still able to see her pretty moss eyes shine with wetness as they pull her out of the house.

I want to kiss her sadness away, but my feet are frozen to the ground. She lifts her head, looking back at me. Her eyes hold a silent plea for help, and I do nothing. My muscles refuse to work, I'm held prisoner in my own mind as I'm forced to watch.

Her brows dip when I do nothing. The cop pats her down, displaying two knives she had hidden on her. Evidence. My heart stills when I see one of the knives is mine. She sucks in a breath, trying to be strong, fighting back the tears.

My chest and ribs are so fucking tight, and still, instead of going to her like I should, I'm thinking about how gorgeous she is. The sight of her has become my kryptonite, and each day I know her it becomes worse.

My heart wants to leap out and attach to hers. She has blinded me, made me weak, sloppy, and the person I've become ignores all logic.

"Max!" she calls for me.

I do nothing but watch her being placed in the back of a cop car, her eyes not moving from mine, then she mouths elephant shoe. My ribs are crushing my internal organs, I should be bleeding out, yet here I stand.

Her hand goes flat on the car window and slowly drags down, making a mark on the clear glass.

I want to move my feet, but I'm locked on her pouty lips and the fact she said she loved me, when I'm the one to blame for everything. God, it's so much easier to believe she said elephant shoe.

The car begins to move, her pretty face removed from my vision, and only then am I able to suck in a breath and force my muscles to move again. I race out the door but everyone's gone except the small-town boy I should dispose of.

"Sienna!" I holler, kicking the dirt at my feet. *What the fuck is wrong with me?*

My fingers claw at my scalp, pulling at the roots of my hair. *I need to fix this.* I turn and bump into Elliot before I even move my feet.

"You need me more than I need you right now, Maximus." That pretty boy exterior morphs into something more sinister.

"Who the fuck are you?" I ask, trying to sidestep him.

I glance behind me, Bram and Jack are cheering with their drinks once again.

"I've been writing you letters."

My feet halt and I give him a better look. No one knows about the letters. I will have to deal with him later. I need to get Sienna out of this. I shake my head, giving him one more look. Fuck! I turn toward my car and the letter-writing freak stays on my heels. He gets into the passenger side without being invited and slams the door the same time as me.

"I've been studying you since I was a teenager. It's why I bought the bar in Oakport, and then decided to move here afterwards. I find you fascinating. You really are a genius."

"What the hell is this? You a serial killer?" I ask, angry at myself that I couldn't find him until he walked up to me.

He laughs—fucking *laughs*—and taps at my shoulder.

"Don't touch me," I seethe. This guy is crazier than me.

"No, I'm not like you. Blood makes me queasy." He shudders at the image he must be thinking about and his face contorts. His lips curl down and his nostrils flare as his eyes widen with disgust. "I want to write a book about you."

I look this guy dead in the eyes and find he's completely serious. For the first time in my life, I'm not the one unfazed, it's this guy. I'm not sure if I'm horrified, impressed, or shocked. He continues, not worried that he's in the car with a serial killer, one who likes to have all his loose ends cleaned up.

"Anyway, Sienna being blamed for your attempted murder is the greatest get-out-of-jail-free card you have. I think we should plan on having the entirety of the club murders put on her. Think about it. Then you can change your M.O. for any new killings. You've switched how you kill twice in your life, might as well switch gears again. This is the perfect opportunity." He jumps with joy in his seat. "I couldn't have planned this better."

He's not even done finishing his last word when I have his throat in my hands and I'm blocking his airway. He smiles at me like this is the best day of his life. There's no fight for his life. I release him and he coughs and wheezes for air.

"I will make you live in history forever," he says, trying to catch his breath.

"I don't care about immortality," I seethe.

"Sure, you do. Your mind is clouded right now. All great killers want what I'm offering you. It's why the Zodiac wrote letters, he wanted the fame, to live in infamy."

My foot is heavy on the gas as I peel out of the parking lot, our bodies tossed backwards into our seats.

"Where are we going?" Elliot asks, vibrating with energy in his seat.

"I'm going to get my girl." I press the gas down harder, taking a turn a little too sharp and leaving marks on the road.

"Don't be stupid. It's what that wannabe, McCain, wants."

I slam on the brakes, throwing our bodies forward. I wish he wasn't wearing a seatbelt and would go through the windshield.

"Yes, I know all about him, too. It's how I found you." He shakes his head like he can't believe his luck.

"I think it's time to tell me everything you know," I say, gripping the wheel tighter than necessary.

"I thought you would never ask," he replies with a smile. "Head to my apartment and I'll show you my journals."

Chapter 31: Sienna

♥

I CAN'T BELIEVE THIS is happening to me. I've been in this small white room with blaring lights for what seems like twenty-four hours.

My eyes are scratchy and keep fluttering closed. I have to force them wide just to stay awake. My father...no, Bram and Jack just watched, the same with Max. He had this odd expression on his face but he didn't move a muscle. He watched me like he does with his textbooks, with hyperfocus and intrigue.

Picture after picture they have shown me, including the so-called bear attack from back in that beach town. It took me an hour to figure out what this all was. I scoff at myself.

And I thought I was smart.

Maximus Mancini does not just kill people, he does it for sport. As in, he's a serial killer. It's not just one or two bodies he's dumped for the mafia. I let a serial killer's hands, which have been bloodied *so* many times, touch me. *Worship* me. I allowed myself to fall for a man who enjoys hurting others and now he's framing me as the killer.

I guess the joke was on me when I took his knife. The knife now in a plastic bag that will be used as evidence.

They keep bombarding me with questions I don't know a single answer to, flinging more pictures and accusations at me. I'm too overwhelmed. It's not like they give me time to think or answer anything in detail.

Each time I tell them it's not me, they have the wrong person, or no...they go off again. They don't ask who I think it is. They aren't looking for the real killer;, they just need a face to pin the crime on so they can pat themselves on the back for a job well done. They want to continue on with their little lives at home, tell everyone what a great job they're doing at keeping the streets safe. I can feel my bitterness ooze out of my pores.

"I'm not a killer," I repeat for I don't remember how many times.

A new cop enters and says something in the other officer's ear. They look at me and the new cop sits down. "Your knife has the DNA of the bear victim on it."

I already figured it wasn't clean. I would bet Max knew I had it the entire time. How long had he been planning this?

"You're not shocked." He states the obvious.

I'm too tired to fake anything at this point. "I just want to go to sleep." I lay my head down, my eyes closing because they're too heavy to stay up.

"Tell us the truth and you can sleep." The voice is smooth and calm, like a lullaby.

"I didn't do it, but if it means I can sleep, sure. I'm your person. You got me." My voice is sluggish, muffled by my head resting on my arms as I hope for sleep to come. My eyes hurt too much to open them again.

I'm pulled up, my feet move with the motion, but I'm too tired to open my eyes to take note of what's happening. I just pray it's sleep.

Chapter 32: Max

♥

Elliot's journals are an omnibus of my life's work. Seeing everything he had was like I was seeing my life from the outside in. He's begging me to tell him everything for his book. I think I might actually do it. It would feel good to talk to someone about it. No more hiding, no more secrets.

I close Elliot's door behind me, looking forward to saving Sienna. The sick and twisted part of this is that I can't wait to see her face when she sees me confess and save her. I finally get to be her savior.

I whistle as I walk down the dark street toward my car. The sound of footsteps has me turning as something is placed over my head. My arms are tied together and I'm lifted off my feet. Each of my limbs convulse in an effort to escape and I'm tossed onto a hard surface.

"Relax, Max, it's us." The cloth over my head is pulled and I stare at my brothers Romeo, Dante, and Savio.

"What the fuck!" I yell, trying to get to my feet, but I'm pushed back down by Savio.

"We can't let you do it," Romeo says, shaking his head. "We need you."

"Do what?" I feign ignorance.

All of them give me the look. "We've been watching you. We saw Sienna get arrested and we can't let you save her."

I turn toward Dante. "You're going to let Sienna rot in prison?" I accuse.

"All of you shut the fuck up!" Romeo hollers, pointing to me. "If you say another word, I'm going to sew your mouth shut."

I open my mouth and Savio hits me upside the head, causing my world to grow dark.

I WAKE UP IN Dante's basement, handcuffed to a table. My eyes slowly blink and my hand reaches to touch the bump on my head but my hands are constricted.

"She confessed."

I stare blankly at Aria Rossi, not realizing someone else was beside me. I repeat her words slowly in my head.

"Impossible," I scoff.

I attempt to rub at my eyebrow, the one that has a line through it because of the saw my father pushed me into as a kid. My fingertips hardly graze it with my hands shackled to the table. I can feel the raised bump of the scar from the butcher saw that brushed against me years ago.

I try to rip my hand from the metal holding me back, but my struggle is useless.

"Romeo!" I holler, standing, trying to lift the table and anything else I can muster. Nothing moves, it only cuts into the flesh along my wrists. My sister-in-law doesn't flinch at my outburst. She gives me this patronizing look, silently scolding me.

Sienna's haunted eyes flash before me as I remember just standing there, doing nothing. I should be jumping around for joy as Aria has reminded me many times already. There will be no chance of anyone looking for me again. This was the reason I wanted a vacation originally. I wanted the papers to stop writing about me, and now I realize I would much rather the media circus than for Sienna to take my place.

I can only imagine the hate running through her at this moment. She probably thinks I set her up, used her for my own benefit, when that was never the case.

For the first time in my life, I loved someone who I didn't pledge loyalty to because we're family. Before Sienna, the only person who had my loyalty was Romeo, not even my other brothers Dante and Savio. To be honest, I hardly remember my younger brothers. Our mother swept them away with her when they were so young and I was fighting to stay alive in my father's world. I'll protect Dante and Savio with my life, but it's not the same. I would destroy the world for Sienna, burn everything to the ground for her and spit on everyone's ashes.

"This can be a good thing." Aria says the same shit everyone else has been. Her boldness continues to shock me and my eyes fly to hers.

"I could snap your neck before you realized I've reached over the table." I speak through clenched teeth, my skin warming at my anger. There's a slight tremble rolling through my body as I try to get myself under control.

Aria doesn't look scared by my outburst. She sits there, quietly studying me like a new rare specimen she wants to dissect.

"In my professional opinion, I think you should lie low until this goes away. It's the mafia way. If you want to show mercy, kill her. She'll feel less pain that way."

Her words are harsh for such a pretty woman. You would never guess that from her soft demeanor, but she didn't get to the top being soft, I suppose. She deals with mafia men all day long.

"Kill her," I scoff, my voice eerily calmer than a moment ago. "That's your suggestion?"

She tilts her head, watching me for any reaction. "Everything in life comes full circle. You were contracted to kill her in the first place, correct? A little prison accident will fly under the radar quite easily."

Aria stands, silently excusing herself, and I'm left sitting there stunned. I'm no coward, and having Sienna take the fall, never mind killing her, seems like a coward's way out. There's nothing noble about it. Not that I'm noble in any way.

I do have honor though. I can't keep my head high or feel good about myself if I do as Aria suggests.

My stomach twists at the thought of Sienna not being in this world. Holy shit, I think I'm gaining a conscience. A gray, almost burned one, but a conscience nonetheless.

For the first time in my life, I don't hear my father yelling at me for being stupid. His voice is the one normally rattling in my brain when I'm stressed out.

I flick my tongue to the top of my mouth to force my teeth to unclench. My father is nowhere to be heard and I'm not sure what to make of it. Maybe, for once, this is the right thing to do. When it comes to Sienna, I'm not a killer. I've always identified myself as one. I'm the black cloud that was shoved in a box and I did as people expected. Everyone sees me as this one-dimensional thing. Not anymore.

A few hours later, Aria is back, still trying to wear me down, but my brothers are nowhere to be seen. Now *those* are cowards, too scared to see my reaction after they ganged up on me.

She sits back down, staring at me point blank, using her serious face.

"Max," she starts. "No amount of money is going to get her off. We need to look at reality. They have hard evidence. So, unless you plan to walk in there and confess..."

I don't even turn my head to look at Aria. I refuse to listen to anyone who doesn't believe in me. And that *was* my idea. I've yet to come up with a better one.

Collecting myself, I focus on not speaking too harshly, trying to get into her head, needing her to listen to what I'm trying to tell her. "Aria, do you remember when you fell in love with your husband?"

Her face softens and I can practically see those invisible hearts floating in her eyes. This is good, maybe she will see reason.

"How would you feel if he was taken away from you?" I ask softly, not wanting to come across too harshly.

She licks her lips, her eyes narrowing toward me. She's taking this personally, I can see those imaginary daggers trying to stab me.

"I'm not threatening, I'm just asking. How did you feel when he was ripped from you all those years ago?" I wait for an answer as we both stare at each other. She's trying to figure me out, or my ulterior motive.

"Like my heart was torn from my chest and I no longer had a purpose," she answers honestly, a sad expression on her face.

"I love Sienna. She's the only thing that matters in my world. If she's gone, my purpose on this Earth is gone with her. Unlock my cuffs. Let me do the first selfless thing I've ever done in my life. Let me put her first."

"That's not the mafia way." She shakes her head. "You know I can't let you go."

"What was that saying your father always said before he died?"

"Family protects family."

I attempt to tap my chest over my heart with my first. "Sienna is in here, she is family."

She tilts her head up, closing her eyes. I think I might have her.

"Please," I beg, my hands making a praying gesture.

Both of her hands go to her cheeks and they hold her chin as she says nothing, but stares at me.

"Tell them I overpowered you. I'll take whatever punishment they give me. Please, do me this one solid."

"Maximus..." My name sounds like a plea on her lips.

I almost have her. "Let me go down by doing one good thing in my life."

She curses in Italian, getting up and pacing the room. More curses fly from her mouth before she storms back to me with a key in her hand. "If you ever tell anyone the truth, I will deny it and kill you in your sleep."

My cuffs are released and I stand. "You are officially my favorite Rossi sister."

I WANT TO SET Sienna's life up before I go away to prison. The first thing I do is find Brute for her. If I can't protect her, he will. It takes mindless hours before finding the correct shelter Brute was tossed into. The moment he sees me, his ears perk up before he jumps at the cage and barks. It's the first time I'm hearing him use his voice.

My stomach is fucking sore from all the invisible punches I've taken to the gut in the last few days.

"He's scheduled to be euthanized this weekend, unless we find him a home," the lady says in a sad voice.

"I'll take him." There's no thinking needed in my decision. Brute was part of Sienna and he's going to stay that way.

Once he's on a leash, I bend down, rubbing at the back of his ears and he pushes his head into my hands. I never realized how much I cut myself off from the world before now. I never needed anyone, ever. I used to prefer to be by myself at all times. With Sienna gone, I'm lonely as fuck.

"You miss her too, huh, Brute?" He does a little whine, agreeing with me.

When did Sienna worm herself into me? I used to go months not seeing anyone. Now, my brothers have become these needy little blood suckers that call me *daily*. One side of my lips hitches up thinking about it. I hate that I like the phone calls.

My father would say needing anyone made you weak, but he's wrong. Being a unit has made us stronger.

One thing I know is that when I go down, it's going to be in spectacular fashion. It will be better than the fireworks on the Fourth of July.

"**A**M I GOING TOO fast? You sure you're getting this down?" I ask Elliot, who's across the kitchen table from me. Not even my family knows all of my secrets, and it feels fantastic to let it out. I didn't even realize I was carrying the weight of it until I unleashed it all. I couldn't stop myself from talking.

His eyes are bright and his fingers are flying over his keyboard a mile a minute. This is the first time I've paused in two hours. Maybe I should have checked in sooner.

"This is gold, keep going."

I speak for a few more hours, until I've told him everything, including all of my secrets. If I'm going to go out, it's going to be with a bang. I want the whole world to know and understand how I work and what I've done. I'll be the greatest serial killer of all time. Elliot wanted a tell-all book and he's going to get his dream. Look at me, making dreams come true all around me.

"Are you really doing this to get your girl back?" he asks at the end, his eyes still scanning over the screen.

"Yes and no," I answer. "It's more redemption of our love, because I'll never see her again once I confess to everything."

"I would've thought you'd pin it all on the cop," Elliot says absentmindedly.

"He never earned the right to go down in history as me. I have something better planned for him. No one fucks with what's mine and lives to talk about it."

This guy has stars in his eyes as he stares at me with his mouth gaped open. He's a bigger fan of my work than Sienna and my family could ever be.

"What are your plans after you publish the book? I won't be around to follow anymore."

He leans back, staring into space. "You've been my life's work. I suppose I'll be lost for a few years until I find someone new." He shrugs. "I'll figure it out."

"That's a good way to get yourself killed. Promise me, no more following serial killers around." I don't know why I say it, other than this guy has grown on me. I feel like the Grinch when his heart starts to enlarge. My hand rubs over mine, feeling the sting.

I'm going to have to kill the cop faster than I plan to get some normalcy back in my life. He will be my last kill and the only one not on record.

"When are you going in? I'd like to be there to be a first-hand witness. It'll make it easier to describe in my book and, let's be honest, this is what the readers will want to know about."

I suck on my bottom lip, thinking. "I have some work to do tonight, but I should be good to go for Thursday morning." The time I've had in Dante's basement allowed me to plan it all out. Two days will give me more than enough time to get everything done.

"What's the ETA for the killing?" he says as if he read my thoughts. I might as well be truthful.

"Tonight, and tomorrow night. Thursday will be a fresh start and that's why I'm heading into the station that morning."

He claps his hands together. "Readers are going to eat that up."

"Be there by eight and you'll see what you need to."

J ACK AND BRAM STARE at me with cocky glares, like they're not afraid of me. *They should be.*

They're tied up in an abandoned warehouse. It's the best I could do with the limited timeframe I have.

"If you wanted Sienna out of your life, why frame her?" I ask harshly, my spit flying into his face. I can hardly keep it together to talk.

"Sienna set herself up," Jack snarls.

Bram, her father, shakes his head. "Sienna ain't even mine. That's why her mother was leaving me. For some asshole country cowboy who thought he could be her savior."

"Don't worry, we killed him, too," Jack smiles, looking like he's walking down memory lane. "I also have a confession, Bram. Sienna is yours. That cowboy never existed." Jack looks to me, then Bram. "I know when I'm at the end of my life, I might as well come clean. I set all that up too."

"You mother fucker!" Bram yells, his knuckles turning white as he grips onto his knee. He can't do much else with how they're tied up.

Jack is on a roll and keeps talking. "Everyone knew he wouldn't allow anyone to touch Sienna. I blackmailed him over the location of his wife's body, so I could finally be the one to shove my cock in her. The plan was to get rid of him after the wedding. I'm the one who cut you off on the highway with his bike, but you never finished the job like you should have. Do you know what happened when I almost died? This guy said the wedding was off, so I did the next best thing. I found Clayton McCain. By then you had already killed a third of our chapter. I thought I'd get rid of both of you. I told McCain where his wife's body was and, well...you know who McCain is."

I turn behind me to see Officer McCain hog tied with tape over his mouth.

I lean back into the chair and study Jack for any sign of a lie while Bram struggles in his bindings.

Holy shit. Jack Pierce set this all up.

I glance at my watch, wishing I'd made more time. I'd love to keep them alive for a month or so, but I only have a few minutes left.

"But why frame her?" I ask again.

"I wanted Bram to suffer as much as possible. It should have been me as president, not him."

Ten minutes later, I had three bodies to dispose of.

Chapter 33: Max

♥

I STAND IN THE shadows across the street, watching the mayhem in front of the police station. I haven't decided how I want to do this yet. Do I go in guns blazing, make them kill me before they toss away the key? Do I walk in proud and say, "Hey fuckers, it's me."? I suppose it will come to me as I go.

Reporters. Hundreds of them line the front of the building. I wasn't expecting a media show. Inwardly, I cringe at the crowd. This is for Sienna. I take one step after another and fight my way through, pushing to the front. I'm all but ignored as heads bob up and down, trying to get a glimpse of something on the inside.

Finally, I make it to the front and find two cops at the doors, trying to keep the chaos to a reasonable level.

"I'm here for Sienna Levine," I announce, ready to go through more detail with all the flashes and cameras at my back. I'm a private person and this is causing my hands to sweat. It's the least I can do.

To my surprise, they open the door. The flashes go crazy as the vultures try to get a glimpse of inside. *What is happening?* I shake my head. Everyone has gone crazy.

Sienna rounds the corner and her eyes widen seeing me. She stops in her tracks, looking cautious and unsure. I can't help myself. I wrap my arms around her, lifting her up. This will be the last time I can hold her. I try to memorize the way she feels. Taking a deep breath, I breathe her in, wishing I could remember this forever. It will be the sound of her voice and her smell that's the first of the memories that go. I hold her so tight, never wanting to let her go. This is worth everything.

"Why are you here?" she asks, squirming in my hold.

It pains me to let her go. My fingers try to keep her until she takes a step out of my grasp.

"I'm getting you out of here," I say quietly, wanting as much time with her as possible before this turns into a circus.

She touches my arm. "If you haven't noticed, I'm out."

My lips flatten as I look from her to the madness outside. "How?"

"The real killer confessed this morning. Do you remember the bartender from Oakport Beach? It was him."

"Impossible," I say, confused.

"That's why all the reporters. I guess he called them and wrote a five-page letter to all of the newspapers. He knows details that have never been released."

My feet shuffle in a circle, trying to comprehend what she's saying. Elliot came here as me?

"He said he won't hide behind newspaper letters like the Zodiac and wants his face to go down in history."

I don't know if I should be insulted or impressed.

"You didn't need to come down here though. My Uber is waiting. Bye Max." She leans in and kisses me on the cheek, her sweet scent wrapping around me, and I don't want to move from it. I watch her walk away from me once again.

This gives me an easy way out. She's alive, safe...I made sure of it. This is the part where she gets erased from my life and I continue on how I was for decades, before my obsession with her started. Letting her walk out of here was the plan, but I thought something would be holding me back. This isn't the plan.

It starts off gradual, my heart thudding like a dull ache before it thunders, tightening its grip and morphing into crippling pain instead of relief. My normal, calm breathing is choppy, like it's being severed by her walking away. She doesn't look back or pause.

Despite my best efforts, none of the raw tenderness—no, pain—is subsiding.

"Can I help you, sir?" The front desk lady is looking at me strangely. "Are you okay?"

I wipe at my sweat-soaked forehead. For the last few years, all I wanted was someone to take the fall for my murders. I searched for the perfect scapegoat.

Am I okay with Elliot taking the blame? I should be, even though he did it underhandedly.

I wait for the jealousy that someone else will be named. I take pride in my work and this is like someone plagiarizing it. Stealing from me.

"I'm fine." I walk out of the station, realizing I don't need the credit. It was never about that, and the reason why I changed how I disposed of the bodies. I never wanted the fame from it, or needed trophies. It was just something I did.

Elliot can have it. Hell, he'll do it better than me, and I have no doubt he will go down in history like he wants. The reporters ignore me, I'm insignificant in their eyes. I prefer that, it was how I was brought up. The only person's eyes I never want to be insignificant in are hers.

Sienna might be done with me, but I'm far from done with her.

Chapter 34: Sienna

THREE DAYS LATER, THERE'S another article about The Butcher in the newspaper, chronicling his last three victims before he turned himself in. My father, Jack, and officer McCain.

I almost laugh at the city celebrating about catching a serial killer that has plagued the United States for twenty years. I down my second beer, feeling sorry for myself, but over what, I don't know. I'm free for the first time in my life. I should be rejoicing. Instead, I feel like crying.

I glance over at my phone, rereading the text message I sent to Max. **Our streets are safe once again. Is it true?** It goes unanswered.

My mother's death anniversary is today. I've never been allowed to go to her headstone, but there's nothing holding me back today.

It takes me a half hour walking around to find the right place. All the other headstones have real or fake flowers around them. They look loved and taken care of, unlike my mother's. I place the bouquet of sunflowers down and use a small fork to dig a hole, placing two sunflower seeds into it before covering it up.

"My father is three rows over from your mother. I wonder if they know each other?" I jump at the timbre of his voice.

Max is standing there in jeans and a white T-shirt. His hands are in his pockets as he looks down at me.

"She probably doesn't like him."

"I don't think anyone ever has," he says, but I refuse to give him any more of my attention. He didn't come and try to see me once I was in custody. He could have prevented everything and did nothing. It shouldn't hurt, but it does. My brain had warped what we really were to each other. I had allowed myself to fall into this dark fairytale where I was the one who got her happily ever after.

My mind drifts back to the police station when he didn't come after me for the second time. Seeing him had my heart bursting with happiness before I realized he wasn't the one who saved me. He stood there, confused to see me walking free.

My life has never been mine to control. My father controlled me for most of it before Max took over. I don't know what a life of my choosing would even look like.

Since Max entered my life, I have smiled more than I ever had, made friends, and felt like someone who I always wanted to be. Now, I'm determined to do it on my terms.

"Why won't you look at me?" He growls, because he's not getting the reaction he wants.

I stand, turning toward him, wanting to say this to his face. "You're a coward."

I stomp past him, my shoulder hitting his arm when he steps toward me but thinks better of it. As he should.

Then I see my dog lying in the grass ten feet from us.

"You stole my dog?" Brute lifts his head, looking at me, but he doesn't move. "He used to like me before you entered and bribed him with ice cream."

"You can have him back."

The audacity of this man.

I turn, marching back to him and pointing my finger into his strong, hard chest. "Does that dog look like he wants to come with me?"

We both turn our heads and Brute is looking at Max, wagging his tail. I'm completely forgotten, like I'm not even here. "See what I mean? You steal everything for yourself."

I can't even be in his presence, he makes me so angry.

"I was coming for you." I stop, unsure if I heard correctly. "That's what I was doing there, at the station."

I scoff out a humorless laugh. "The Max I know never wants to be in the spotlight. Looks like it worked out for you and you get to continue walking around among the shadows like you prefer. You're off the hook. I don't need you anymore."

My voice comes out loud and strong when I feel nothing like that. I want to cry, and eat ice cream, and fall into myself until this black cloud that's hovering over my head disappears.

I 'VE WALKED BY THRONE of Sin every day for the last two weeks. I miss my best friend, I miss my job, and there's even a part of me that misses those bitchy girls.

"Hey, New York. We've missed you around here." The bouncer greets me as I walk closer. "You coming in today?"

I place my hands in my front pockets. "I'm thinking about it. Is Dante in?"

The bouncer's eyes light up. "He is. And if you go in, you're going to make me a hundred bucks."

"What?"

"Girl, you have been missed like hell, and we see you walking by. Dante had you never coming back, Demi had you coming back a week ago, and Shelby bet tomorrow. Today is my bet," he says proudly.

I scratch at my temple. "I'm not going to be thrown out the moment I step inside, right?"

"Sienna, go in." He gives me a look.

I suck in a breath. It's now or never. "Looks like you are a hundred dollars richer." I smirk, but in reality, I also don't want Shelby to win the bet.

It's strange to see someone else bartending. I walk by them, hoping not to be noticed, and knock on Dante's door.

"It's open."

I hesitantly push the door open with one finger until I'm standing in the small open space between the door and the frame.

Dante sits there, his face like stone, looking angry, yet void of emotion, as he says, "I thought we were adults and promised each other we couldn't go crying, broody, or fire each other?" I study him for a beat, it's impossible to get a read on what's going through his head right now.

"In my defense, I didn't promise I wouldn't steal from you." Might as well talk about this.

He levels me with a look. "I knew the night you started it."

I flinch, my eyes growing wide. "Why didn't you say anything? The guilt was killing me."

"I didn't care. I could have transferred the money back to myself at any time. And I thought it was funny that Max thought he was the big man trying to solve a case. I know everything about my club and he thought I had no idea. So, I just let Max do his thing. What I didn't expect was you two being a thing. Max, really?"

"Not anymore. We're done."

Dante doesn't look convinced. "Does he know that?"

"Trust me, he'll get the hint soon enough."

"Fuck, I missed that attitude of yours." He stands and walks over, giving me a hug. I'm taken off guard and speechless. Dante has never hugged me, not of his own accord. I know he's only tolerated me touching him before. This is a big deal. My eyes blur with happy tears that I have my friend back. I squeeze him harder, and that's Dante's breaking point. He immediately lets go of me and steps back.

"Friends?" I ask.

"No." He shakes his head. My heart drops, along with my smile. "We're family." My shoulders relax instantly. "Cause I could have used my best friend when I found out I had a daughter."

I give him a shy smile. I can't help the guilt that twists my heart to hear he needed me and I wasn't around. "I'm sorry, Dante."

"Stop being a girl, we're good. I'm over it now that you're back. When can you start again?"

"Bartending and bookkeeping?" I ask, excitement building in my limbs at the idea of getting my old job back.

He laughs. "Bartending. No bookkeeping. No offense."

I can't fault him for that. "I hear ya."

I open my mouth to say sorry again, but he puts up his hand. "Don't you dare say sorry again, or I'll retract the job offer."

"Thank you."

He goes to sit back down. "Now go. I have work to do."

I appreciate how Dante didn't make this weird, and I'm beyond grateful for his forgiveness. I walk out of the strip club and spot Max in the corner. He sometimes hides from me, other times he stays in clear view like he wants to remind me he's still there watching, but my skin refuses to let me forget him.

My skin warms and my heart tugs like it does every time I sense he's around, and it's *all* the time.

It's impossible to forget him or push him out of my mind with the constant reminders. He refuses to get that he stomped on my heart and tore it to shreds when he was willing to let me take the fall for him. I could have ratted him out, I had so many opportunities, but I didn't. The thought never occurred to me when it should have.

I held his future in my palm and I chose to ruin my life by staying quiet. I can't chance being hurt like that again.

Chapter 35: Max

♥

I DON'T GO ANYWHERE unless Sienna is in my view, whether it's on my cameras or I'm watching from afar. She consumes me more than ever.

"I need you to go out of town." Romeo interrupts my viewing and places his hand over my screen as I actively try to ignore him.

"Nope." My molars grind against each other.

Romeo crosses his arms over his chest. "Max, this is your job. You're The Butcher."

"I'm not leaving her. And the guy in jail is The Butcher, I'm just Max," I say pointedly.

"This is an order," Romeo bellows. He's always so emotional when it comes to me. The vein in his forehead is protruding like it always does when he gets angry.

"My heart isn't in it." I shrug. "I've lost my mojo and I don't trust myself to not make a mistake that will come down on me and the family."

He's staring at me, open mouthed. "This isn't an option."

I lay my phone down, my eyes wanting to stay glued to Sienna, but I force them upon my ugly brother. "I can't."

"You have to and will," he seethes.

I'm impressed with my outer calmness. "I want more in life, Romeo. For once, let me take care of my life before I'm forced to deal with the family. I've never asked for much ever. Please, grant me this."

"She's made you weak. Can't you see this?" His eyes search mine, probably looking for the brother he thinks he's lost.

My anger rises and I stand. "You get to have a family, a wife. I remember a time they made *you* weak. Why won't you allow me the same opportunity? Sienna made me human. I just want what you have." There I said it. He stares at me, not saying a word.

"Well, you're doing a shit job at trying to get your girl back."

It takes a second to realize he's not giving me shit about helping the family. "I'm doing everything I can do to get her back," I scoff.

"Bullshit. You're staying away from her because you're scared of rejection. It's the same reason you work by yourself and refuse to do anything even remotely family like. You're scared of being rejected like how Dad rejected you his whole life."

Fuck, the truth is painful. My jaw clamps and my molars grind against each other. My fingers tingle, wanting to cut my brother's throat.

"There's that fire I love seeing." He slaps me on the shoulder and I realize he was riling me up on purpose. "Now, go get the fucking girl."

I WATCH SIENNA GET on the fucking plane. She thinks she's being so sneaky, wearing a wig and sunglasses too large for her face. She hands over her passport with a fake name. I almost killed Dante when he told me he gave her a fake passport. If it wasn't for Demi, I would've never learned where she was planning to travel. Thank goodness Demi loves people being in love.

The doors on the plane close and my cockpit closes with finality. I would love nothing more than to walk out and watch the expression on her face, but I refrain. I have to play the slow game to win her back.

We arrive in Alberta, Canada. It's July and should be hot, but it's raining and tiny blood suckers are biting at my ankles as I watch Sienna get into an Uber. My hand swats at the mosquitoes and some blood is smeared on my skin.

She holes up in a small little tourist town, surrounded by mountains. This would be the easiest place to dispose of bodies and it reminds me a little of Oakport Beach. Minus the ocean, add in the mountains and a few more tourists, but the feeling you get is the same.

I make note of every man who eye fucks her. If they so much as talk to her, I'm liable to go on a killing spree.

Chapter 36: Sienna

♥

I THOUGHT I WOULD be happy starting over. I now bartend in this super cute Canadian-themed restaurant. Luckily, I was able to get an apartment with picturesque views of the snow-covered mountain peaks. I get to walk to work, everyone is friendly. I've even made a new friend, but my heart isn't in it.

When I'm making drinks, the minutes fly by. The moment I stop it's like each second is stretched into an hour. I should be living life on a high right now. I have everything I wanted: a new start, a friend, a job I love, and the views are breathtaking. However, it's when I rest, or late at night, when my mind wanders to the Mancinis.

To be specific, Max fucking Mancini. He's a coward who has no personal boundaries or concept of right or wrong. I huff out a breath, realizing the biggest red flag is that he enjoyed killing. He was raised to be a serial killer. It's a damn good thing red is *not* my favorite color, because that flag is waving high all around me.

I just never thought Max would let me sit in jail to take the fall for his doings. I trusted him to save me, protect me, and he did neither.

My body shivers for no reason as I hike up the raised land that's more like a massive hill than a mountain to get to the other side of the Bow River to watch the waterfall. Like every other time I had this sensation, my feet stop and I look around. Once again, I force myself to keep going. Dante promised me he wouldn't tell Max where I was going. I'm working under a different name now. Sienna Levine no longer exists. I erased her.

I'm breathing less heavily on this hike as the waterfall comes into view and I take a seat on one of the benches. Tourists take pictures of the water cascading down the rocks behind their selfies, people are walking and riding bikes all around me.

I hate that I feel insignificant. Nothing would change if I disappeared and no longer sat on this bench. It's what happened when I left Texas. Nothing. Everything and everyone went on doing what they have always done. I was a blip on the radar that never shocked anyone into missing me.

I miss Max.

Holy fucking Hell. That thought just exploded into my head and I can't push it out. I'm going to need something stronger than the water in my bottle. Maybe I'm delirious from the overexertion of the hike? I check my forehead, and this time there isn't even a splatter of sweat. I'm going crazy, that has to be the answer. I heard there's a psych ward for people a few hours from here...maybe I should check myself in.

My shoulders deflate and I lean back as if I'm trying to become one with the bench. I glance over, watching people board an orange boat that floats down the river in the opposite direction of the waterfall.

My spine stiffens. I swear I see Max standing there watching me. I have to look away and look back to be sure. The figure is gone.

I need to pack and leave. I stand and a bike almost runs me over as they zoom in front. "Sorry!" is called out as they continue on their way.

That's when I decide I refuse to be on the run every time I get spooked. Maybe I should call Dante and double check he never told his brother anything. Damn it. I miss him too. And Throne of Sin. Even the bitchy girls there. They were slowly starting to come around to me.

I think they aren't used to people staying long in their lives and it takes a long time for them to trust that a person will stick around before they put any effort into being friendly.

I proved them right by leaving.

I GLANCE UP THE wooden stairway that leads back up and over the small mountain and my thighs instantly throb in protest. I won't be going back that way. My hands push off my legs, which have become stiff from sitting, and head toward the windy road beside it.

Maybe a car will hit me, putting me out of my misery. A car comes around at a snail's pace, expecting pedestrians on the road. They even give me a small wave as hello as they pass. That won't be happening here.

The main road in town is closed for vehicles as I walk down the middle of it to stay out of the crowd. I venture back to the sidewalk for the liquor store and grab a six-pack of Molson Canadian beer, cracking the tab before I hit my apartment building. That same shiver as before dances down my spine. I'm starting to hate-yet-relish the feeling.

Groaning, I take a large gulp of the beer and head up toward my little apartment-style condo.

I kick off my shoes as I enter my place. This is the first time I've ever had a place I could say was mine. Before, my father owned the apartment I had, but only because I refused to stay at his clubhouse. Then Max set me up in the apartment.

I drop my empty beer on the counter and take my time downing the rest of the six pack while sitting on my couch, overlooking the mountains.

Like from earlier, I swear I see Max, this time in the shadows of my apartment. I really can't get him out of my head. Sighing heavily, I close my eyes, allowing the alcohol to drag me off to a restless sleep, even though it's early afternoon.

I wake up, my hand tingling, but I can't move it. My eyes fly open to realize I'm tied down on my bed. "What the..." Max's rough voice cuts through my words.

"Hello, Sienna. You need to listen or I'll gag you."

My throat works the collecting saliva down my throat as my eyes try to pierce him with tiny stabs all over that gorgeous face of his.

"I'm sorry," he murmurs with finality.

He takes a seat at my feet, his hands touching and testing the rope while the bed dips beneath his weight.

"I wanted to save you from jail. Romeo tricked me and had me locked away so I couldn't take your place. The moment I was free, I should have come to you. I fucked up." He makes a *tsk*ing sound and shakes his head. "But I want you to know that the time between was me trying to protect you. In one night, I had your father and husband disappear." He glares as if the word husband tastes like acid in his mouth. "I wanted to have my story out there so no one could tangle my words and try to say it wasn't me. I had no idea that the person I told my story to would take the fall for me. He stole my grand entrance, but I was also relieved because that meant I could spend the rest of my days with you."

"How chivalrous of you." I grit my teeth.

"I miss you," he confesses, his voice soft and cautious, and his eyes shine with sincerity.

My body tenses and I rest my head on the pillow, refusing to meet his eye. If I wasn't vibrating with anger over being tied up, I might go back to sleep and pretend he wasn't here.

"I fucked up." His tone is careful and he hesitates for a moment. "I've never loved anyone other than Romeo before. I'm trying to learn how I need to be acting. I even read some of your favorite books to see what the dudes in them do."

"You can't take someone else's fictional life and try to make it your own, Max. You don't have a heart. If you did, you would know what you need to do because the answer lies in there."

His hand rests on my foot, his thumb brushing back and forth. "I'm going to win you back, Sienna. And when I do, I'm flying us back home."

"Home. I don't have one of those," I scoff.

"You do. It's in Texas." I glance up at him and see him rolling his eyes with a frown before he says, "Dante misses his best friend."

A sarcastic laugh bubbles out with his reaction. "I like him more than you."

"Maybe, for now." He frowns again. "And I'm forcing myself to be okay with it."

We're both silent for a long minute before he speaks again. "No one at Throne of Sin has been the same since you left. Even Romeo, who never regrets anything, is seeing he fucked up too. You're part of my family now, and with you leaving, it's left a gap that's unable to be filled."

More silence.

"I'm so sorry I hurt you, baby. I'm not leaving until you forgive me."

"Max, you can't stalk me for the rest of your life."

"I can't let you go, because you're in here." He bangs on his chest above his heart. "You can go on with your life. I won't even kill any man who tries to make you happy. I'll be in the shadows, only to make sure you're safe."

"Max." My tone is one of warning. "We both know that this might last a week. Romeo will call you home."

He shakes his head, giving me an indulgent smile. "I quit. I can't do my job when the only thing I can think about is you." He looks out my window. "But you might be right. My shadowing you might only last a little while before he sends someone after me. There's only one way out, and it's through a casket."

He unties my feet. I stretch my legs out and he kisses me on my forehead before untying my arms.

"Goodbye, Sienna." His tone sounds so sad and final it has my heart speeding up.

I watch his back retreat, listening to my door open and close. My fists pound on the mattress and I let out a frustrated scream. *The nerve of that man!*

Chapter 37: Sienna

♥

I CAN FEEL MAX'S eyes on me the entire shift at work. I even flirt with a few of the male servers to see if he'll keep his word. When they return to the restaurant the next day, I feel guilty for putting their lives in danger.

After my shift, I walk down the winding road to the waterfall. The road is dark with no street lights, and it's raining again. Water drips off my face down my hoodie and the fabric of my jeans clings to my skin from the dampness.

Car lights illuminate the road but I don't step closer to the shoulder. Everyone here seems to have no problem going around pedestrians at a snail's pace. My toes are feeling the cold rain and puddles are becoming hard to miss.

The lights from the car blind me and their speed hasn't slowed, but a heavy hand pulls me in when a car gets too close. "Stop pushing my buttons, Sienna." A warmth covers my body at the sound of his rough voice.

"I have no idea what you're talking about. You said you would leave me alone."

Darkness blankets us when the car takes the light with them.

"No, I said I would stay to protect you." His other hand's thumb and forefinger circle my earlobe. I don't push him away like I should, and he doesn't release me. "You are the only thing to ever make me feel alive, like I was worth more than my sins. You hold my heart and soul now."

His words should mean nothing to me, but they fill my heart with longing. "I can't love a man like you."

"I know, baby. That's why I'm repenting by making sure you're safe. You're my salvation."

I can't catch my breath as his words feather past my ear. I refuse to allow my eyes to water. He doesn't deserve my emotions. I turn to glare at him, ready to voice my annoyance with him still touching me, when he turns me in his arms and kisses my lips. It's short and sweet before he disappears into the darkness of the night.

How can I feel anything for a man like him? He did me so incredibly wrong. He's a bad man. But then why does my heart beat for him? It refuses to turn off and reject him.

I stomp away, frustrated at myself.

The next night, I go on a walk through the woods. There's no light pollution, making it blacker than I've ever experienced. My heart speeds up the deeper I go as my body waits in anticipation for Max to show himself.

I've become an adrenaline junkie for these moments when he appears out of the shadows like a wraith. The ground is wet from the rain and each step is muddy, but I continue on. The muck has my feet slipping slightly but I'm able to continue. I even fake fall, but no Max.

I allow for a branch to swing back and hit me. Nothing but a sore forehead is what I get. The sound of voices reaches me from somewhere deep in the trees, growing louder as I push forward with each slippery step.

"Well, well. Hello, pretty lady." The male's voice stretches past the trees before I see the two men. My pulse accelerates.

"What are you doing out here all alone?" the other one asks.

I look around for Max, my feet stopping as I try to feel him. I get nothing.

"There's been sightings of a bear near here. How about we walk up with you." It's the way they're looking at me that has my alarm bells going off. *Max...*

"I'm good to continue by myself." I give a tight smile and continue, but they turn with me.

"Nonsense. We'll come."

My heart is trying to break through my ribs. What was I thinking, hiking alone at night? I wish I could have smacked myself before I had this stupid idea.

"You heard the lady." Max's stern tone comes from behind me. I step back until I feel his chest at my back.

He doesn't need to tell the men twice. They leave in a half jog and slide down about ten feet of mud before they continue out of sight, the darkness gobbling them up.

I turn into his arms. I've missed his touch. "You look relieved to see me," he whispers, kissing my neck. My eyes close and I lean into him. I'm so tired of fighting this.

"Don't be ridiculous," I scoff and he chuckles. We're chest to chest, his arms wrapped around me in a hug. His heart is pounding as fast as mine.

"All I ever wanted was to be your hero, but I couldn't do that without being your villain, too." He kisses my cheek. "I don't know how not to be a villain when that's all I've ever been. I tried to be different with you. I'm not used to failing at anything. I'm sorry I failed at loving you. It haunts me every day. I'm trying to let you go, because I know that's what you want, but I don't know how." He takes my hand and places it on his racing heart. "You're in here and I don't want to erase you. I don't even know how. I've tried."

My eyes tear up with his truthfulness. The emotion of his deep, dark-blue eyes has my tears slipping over my dark lashes. "I love you so much it hurts, Sienna." His words are choked up and he clears his throat but never looks away. His eyes stay pinned on mine.

"I never wanted to be the one who made you cry." His hands cup my face. "Tell me to leave. Tell me you hate me. Tell me that I can never be your hero. I'll leave. Or at least I'll try to. I want to do one good thing by you, but I need to hear it from you."

"What if I can't?" I ask, my broken voice hardly audible.

"I love you so much, Sienna." He kisses my lips.

I do the opposite of what I should, I melt into his embrace. I hate how well he kisses, but most of all I hate how he feels like home. My chest flutters and my heart cracks, wanting to let him in.

"I love you, too," I whisper.

Max kisses me harder, pulling me snug against him. Our tongues twirl around each other, as if fighting for dominance, fighting to keep our love alive.

Max sweeps me off my feet, walking us back to my place. The door slams behind us, but all I can see is the deep need he's looking at me with. My hand cups his stubbled, sharp jaw, and I inhale a shaky breath.

No matter his faults, all I can see is the good in him. Our feet stumble as he reaches to rid me of my shoes and he kicks his off, all while keeping me his hold on me.

"You are the best thing to ever happen to me," he murmurs, kissing me. He drops me on my bed, but I don't have a moment to catch my breath because he's crawling toward me. His hands pull at the button of my jeans before he's pulling my pants off me.

There is something mesmerizing about the way he looks at me when he becomes hyper focused.

My hands fumble to undo his pants as his lips glide down my neck.

He steps back, eyes on me, and rids himself of his pants before pulling his shirt off too. His cock stands at attention, begging for me to touch it. I sit up, pulling my shirt off next, and unclasp my bra, allowing it to fall off with ease.

He smirks. "You seem to be as impatient as I am." His eyes fall from my eyes down my body with an appreciative look. "Fuck, I love your body."

"Max," I plead, wanting his hands back on me.

He grips my ankles and pulls me to the edge of the bed before placing a kiss between my legs. I shiver at the light sensation. His hand glides up, squeezing my breasts. His motions alternate between flicking my clit with his tongue and rolling my nipples. He works my body into a frenzy, needing, wanting him more than I ever have.

I push my hips into him, feeling that light sensation that is curling its way into me before it unleashes like an explosion.

My fingers go to thread through his hair but he moves. "Nope, you're not coming yet. I want us to go at the same time."

A frustrated groan escapes my pouty lips and I watch as his dick turns harder. My frantic breathing has my chest pushing my tits up and down, and Max is watching them like he would love nothing more than to fuck them.

Crawling over me, he cages my head between his forearms and kisses me slowly, teasingly. I nip at his lip, wanting more, and a soft chuckle vibrates against my lips.

"What is it you're hoping for?" he asks between his polite kisses. Nothing I want him to do with me is polite.

"I want you to fuck me like you're never going to see me again." He pauses at my words.

"Will I get to see you again after this?" I hate the vulnerability in his tone, but understand why it's there.

"Only if you make me forget my name while you fuck me." My hand pulls at his neck, kissing him demandingly. To my delight, he reciprocates and kisses me like a starved man.

He lines his cock up and the tip brushes against my pussy. Each of his small moves has his head brushing against where I want it most.

I move my hips, tilting my pelvis, wanting his cock to be buried in me. The vibration of a chuckle leaves him before his cock is deep inside me.

"Yes, Max," I moan.

I match each of his thrusts, holding onto him like a life preserver. My nipples brush against his chest hairs and I can feel the way his heart speeds up. He kisses my neck, each brush of his touch driving me wild.

I can't help it, I'm so in love with this man. I moan louder feeling my body soar closer to the edge.

Max's movements are becoming faster, harsher, with a determined purpose. My eyes roll behind my eyelids before the overwhelming feeling of my orgasm washes over me. "Max!" I cry out, clinging to him with all my might as my body is pushed off the deep end.

"Fuck, Sienna, I can feel you clutching my cock so fucking tightly." He pushes his dick in deep and rolls his hips against me, hitting my clit and causing my orgasm to linger longer than normal.

"I love you." Max collapses onto me, holding himself up by his forearms.

My smile widens on my face as I open my eyes. He's staring into my eyes like the world revolves around me.

"I love you so much it hurts," I whisper, leaning up to kiss him.

"You are what makes my life worth it," he confesses, grinning at me.

"You will always be worth my love," I say, meaning it with my whole heart. I have no doubt that our love will conquer all and I'll be happier than I ever have been before.

Chapter 38: Max

♥

I HOLD ON TO Sienna's shoulders as I guide her into Throne of Sin with a blindfold wrapped around her flawless face. Her steps are hesitant, but she vibrates with an excited energy I've come to love. Everyone who loves and adores her is in this space. I'm in awe of how easily she has made everyone fall in love with her. I shouldn't be. After all, she captured *my* heart the moment I laid eyes on her. It's her aura that pulls everyone in, whether you want to be or not.

Much to my annoyance, Dante was all too happy to help me organize this little get together and willingly closed the strip club on his busiest day of the week. His grin is the biggest of everyone here and he's the first person I see as we enter the main area.

The room is silent as everyone from Throne of Sin and my family wait with suspended excitement to see Sienna's shocked face at seeing them. Each and every face genuinely lights up with anticipation.

This is what she deserves. A family.

It has me letting my guard down slightly and a smile forming on my face. Slipping the silk from her eyes, she's greeted with a welcome home sign and everyone yelling, "Surprise!"

"What is this?" Her hands cup her face as she looks around in shock. Her moss-green eyes sparkle when she looks back at me. That look is everything. It has my heart skipping a beat. Sienna makes everything in my world worth it.

Thank you, she mouths, her eyes sparkling at me like I'm the center of her universe. We stare at each other, her dismissing everyone but me. It's moments like these that claw deep into my soul. Pure warmth covers my body and I've never been more content.

Dante pulls at her hand, turning her from me into his embrace. My smile strains, becoming forced, and my fingers want to wrap around his neck. I hate anyone touching her. She looks over his shoulder at me and gives me a wink like she knows I'm trying to control myself. I force my shoulders to relax, not wanting to take anything away from this night. Tonight, it's all about her and not about my sensuous need to keep her close.

The girls from the club are next in line. Everyone is surrounding her, pushing me out of the way. I leave the circle and sit at the bar. I watch Romeo stand in front of her and they pause, the room growing silent before he grabs her in an awkward hug and says something in her ear. I stand, waiting for her to grow stiff, but she relaxes and says something back that makes him laugh.

Sitting back down, I lean over the bar to fill myself a beer. Sienna is swarmed by everyone who loves her, she doesn't need me right now. She hasn't even looked my way once since Dante pulled her away. I force myself to look away, opening my textbook pretending to be engrossed in it. It doesn't stop my mind from wandering like it typically does. I stare at the pages while trying to listen to every word said to her.

"Why are you sulking into your beer by yourself?"

I glance up and give Sienna a half smile. She truly is my angel. "I'm studying."

"No, you're not. You're pouting." She's the most beautiful person I've ever set my eyes on and I love her ability to call me out.

"Everyone is here for you, not me. I'm happy to give everyone their moment with you before I sweep you off your feet and hide you away until I decide I've had my nightly fill." That may be one of the truest statements I've ever said.

Her hand touches mine and links our fingers together. "Thank you for organizing this."

I puff out a sound. "I did nothing, this was all your best friend."

She laughs, her eyes crinkling at me like she can see right through me. "Dante already let the cat out of the bag. You did all of this."

I shrug. "It was nothing. All I had to say was that you were coming home and everyone jumped on board, taking over."

She bends down, capturing my lips with hers. I could kiss her forever. I swear her lips have mind control abilities because everything ceases to exist when I'm kissing her.

"Thank you." She bats her gorgeous greens at me and pulls me away from the bar. "You know, when I first saw you at the bar, I thought you were this sexy nerd."

"Sorry I disappointed you."

She shakes her head. "You far exceeded my expectations. I love everything about you, even your darkness. I like knowing no one can fuck with me because you will always protect me."

I bend down, kissing her, wrapping her in a protective hold. The room erupts into catcalling in the background. It has me smiling through our kiss, and we're both breathless when I finally release her. Sienna sways, being lightheaded from my touch. It has me puffing out my chest.

I was going to wait to do this later, but that need to mark her has me deciding now is the perfect time.

When she finds her bearings, I drop down on one knee.

Her eyes widen in disbelief.

"Sienna, will you give me my happily ever after by marrying me?" I pull out a ring from my pocket, holding it out for her. My hand stays suspended in the air as her eyes dart from me to the ring. Her mouth is gaped open in the perfect *O* shape that would allow my cock to slide in perfectly.

Insecurities flutter their way through my nerves as I watch her mouth open and close like her voice gets caught in her throat. I shift in my stance, hating the silence surrounding us. This is not the reaction I was going for. Maybe I read the situation wrong. I slowly get up from my feet, hoping to play this off as no big deal, but my heart surges with excessive thumping, trying to claw its way out of my chest.

"It's too early..." I say, my hand lowering.

"Yes!" Her words are pushed out into a scream. "Yes!"

Relief settles over my entire being. My chest releases the breath I was holding and I slip the ring onto her shaky fingers before pulling her into a hug. "You scared the shit out of me, baby."

Her hand cups my jaw. "I love you."

My forehead touches hers and I breathe in that sweet scent of hers. Everything about her calms me in a way nothing has ever been able to do.

"Everyone in this room loves you, Sienna. They would move the world for you. Even my family won't accept me without you now. This is your home, *our* home. We all can't be born into families we like or would ever choose. Everyone here wants you to be part of this family they've created, and it's so much stronger than anything we could have been born into. If you want this, so do I, and I will do anything to keep it if it means you're happy."

"All I need is you," she whispers.

I can feel the fur from Brute wiggling his way between us. Sienna laughs, rubbing him behind his ears.

"Dante said you can start to bring Brute to work with you, and he can stay by the counter."

Dante squeezes my shoulder and stands beside us. "We decided if you said no, we can get rid of this schmuck for you." He's looking at Sienna and I can't tell if he's joking.

I elbow him, although it's the least violent thing I'd like to do. Sienna waves her hand for him to see and he says, "I'm kidding, Max." *Was he though?* "Welcome to the family, Sienna. Just remember, no returns on this big guy."

"Stop flirting with my woman!" I step between them, half joking. Everyone is offered a glass of champagne and the room erupts in the clinking of glass, even though that's typically reserved for weddings.

I tighten my hold on her, tilting my face toward hers. Our lips brush against each other and I plan to do a soft sweet kiss, but her arms wrap around my shoulders and her mouth opens for my demanding tongue. I remember a time when having her in my arms was a fantasy. Having all of her is surreal and I have to remind myself that this is my life, our life. As if it pains me, I slowly release her, loving the way her eyes are clouded over with lust and desire. The world will now know that Sienna Levine is my woman.

Epilogue: Max

♥

4 months later

My tolerance for people is shot after this fucking zoo of a wedding. Everyone is hugging Sienna, crying on her shoulder as if they never saw two people in love before. If I'm forced to stand here any longer, I'm not responsible for my actions. It will be all their faults.

"You guys can come stay with us." Each of my brothers have offered their homes to us while we build our own place. Romeo knows I hate each of their offers, but smirks at me like there's nothing I can do about it.

"I thought Sienna was a loose end that needed to be dealt with? I'm not leaving her alone near you," I grumble, knowing now that we're married my brother would never harm her. She's family now.

"I already apologized to her over that small detail. And as a sorry, I'm allowing you to work out of town for half the year."

I smile at the thought of that. Elliot allowed me to buy his tavern in Oakport Beach from him. Sienna and I decided we will split our time here and there while running the local pub. We'll see how long we last in such a small town, but crazier things have happened.

The need to kill isn't the same anymore. The urge is still greatly there, but only when it comes to protecting Sienna. In the last four months, I've only taken on necessary jobs from Romeo. He's happier and less stressed now that I don't go rogue on him. It's a win for all.

Sienna touches my hand, my eyes naturally finding hers. No one has to tell me that I'm one lucky bastard. She's a hundred times out of my league but I'm the one she fell in love with. I can never get enough of her pretty smile, alluring moss-green eyes, or her sassy attitude. My eyes drop, taking her in, in her white wedding dress. Damn, I want to rip off that dress and my hands want to dig into those curves I love so much.

"Stop those naughty thoughts of yours. You still owe me a dance." On cue, the music rolls through the inside garden-like venue. I grab Sienna's hand and lead her to the dance floor. It's only family here tonight, creating a close and intimate setting. Something I used to think I would hate, but it's oddly settling.

"Did you see the newspaper article on my father's old motorcycle club?" she asks while I lead her around the dance floor.

"What article?" I play dumb.

"The whole club has decided to leave the area. The crime rate is down twenty percent from previous years."

"Strange." I dip her, loving the way she follows my lead and holds onto me tighter.

"You wouldn't know anything about that would you?" she asks, lifting a perfectly manicured brow.

I hold her closer, breathing in her sweet scent. "I heard they felt like it was a bad omen since most of their chapter ended up missing."

"Hmmmmm..." is her response, knowing damn well it was me that forced them out. She rests her head on my chest. "I'm not sure if I ever thanked you for upheaving my life. I was never brave enough to leave, and each day I'm grateful that I caught your eye."

"I'm the lucky one, baby." I place a kiss under her ear on her neck, enjoying the way she shivers her response.

The song ends too soon for my liking and we retreat toward my brothers. I always thought I was more like a lone wolf, but Sienna is starting to have me believe I love the company of my family more than I admit. It was the voice of my deceased father that continually pushed me away, thinking that I was inferior and they wouldn't accept me because of my enjoyment of the dark side of our business. I'm realizing this is not true at all. They all embrace me without reservation.

"Husband, take me home," Sienna's voice is husky as she looks me up and down with satisfaction.

She doesn't have to ask me twice.

I will stop at nothing to keep that smile on her face.

She is my everything.

Author note:

I CAN'T BELIEVE THIS is my twenty second book! I started Throne of Obsession over two years ago, before I even started to write Sinful Queen. I loved Max from my Dark Mafia Sins series (you see him in his brother Romeo's book, Sinful Kisses) and wanted to write his story so bad. His voice started to scream at me with furry but then suddenly stopped. I had written about twenty percent of his book before I was forced to put it on the shelf. Hence the reason I went on to write a few more books, and it never seemed like the right time to pick his story up again, until earlier this year. This time I felt like I could give his voice the story he needed, and Throne of Obsession was born. I hope you loved this story as much as I did writing it. This is the last book in my mafia throne series.

If you would like to help an author out and support me, I would appreciate it if you left an honest review for Throne of Obsession. Each and every review helps.

Be on the lookout for my new series in 2024.

Other books by Emily Bowie

DARK MAFIA SINS SERIES (**Dark Romance / Mafia**)

Sinful Vow: (Luca & Aly) kidnapping, forced marriage

Sinful Daughter : (Aria & Theo) enemies to lovers, mafia princess/cop,

Sinful Kisses: (Gia & Romeo) enemies to lovers

Sinful Bodyguard: (Fin and Luna) A mafia bodyguard romance

Sinful Queen, (Katrina and Demetri) A secret baby, mafia romance coming this August 2022

Each book can be read as a standalone

Mafia Thrones (Dark Romance/ Mafia)

Throne of Diamonds: (Savio & Charlotte) arranged marriage, strong female lead romance

Throne of Sin: (Dante & Demi) second chance romance

Throne of Obsession: (Max & Sienna) Stalker, mafia romance

Oakport Beach Series (Small Beach Town / Romantic Comedy)

Crashing Hearts (Crash & Piper's story) Summer fling/ falling for your boss romance

Southern Hearts (Danger & Haven's story) Friends to Lovers romance

Wild Hearts (Frankie & Deacon's story) enemies to lovers

*each of these books is a standalone and can be read in any order.

Steele Family Series (Small Town / Romantic Suspense)

Stolen Moments (book #1) (Shay & Luke) Brother's best friend romance

Moonlight Moments (Book #2) (Kellen & Sloan) Insta love (fling to forever)

Bittersweet Moments (book #3) (Brax & Raya) Secret baby

Whisky Moments (book #4) (Rhett & Camilla) Enemies to lovers, Rock star romance

All books are designed to be read as a standalone. Although, characters do have a reoccurring role in each book.

Box set of the Steele Family series:

Standalones: (Small Town / Romantic Suspense)

Pretty, Twisted Lies (Kiptyn's book):

Kiptyn McGrath:

Kellie Dare was never meant to be mine. We existed in two different worlds. Mine was dark, dangerous, and unpredictable. Her's held prestige, wealth, and promise. I was never her white knight but allowed her to believe it until the day she forgot she was mine. I quickly became the villain who would stop at nothing to keep her.

Bennett Brothers Series (Small Town/Romantic Suspense)

Recklessly mine (book #1) second chance love

Recklessly Forbidden (book #2) small town romance

Recklessly Devoted (book #3) enemies to lovers, next-door neighbors

Box set of the Bennett Brothers:

Thank you

♥

THE JOURNEY OF WRITING a book involves a community of people, who supports and helps an author throughout the process.

Thank you to everyone who has picked up Throne of Obsession and has taken the time to read it. You are the best! I would love if you left a review with your thoughts. Every review is so helpful.

Thank you to the following:

Give Me Books: for helping with my cover reveal and release.

Bloggers and influencers: without word of mouth, Throne of Obsession may have never found its way into a readers hands and I thank you for everything you do.

My beta readers: Chanel, Linda and Krista. Ladies, you all add so much insight into my books. You help add details I have overlooked, and give me insight in how to make each story the best it can be. Thank you!

David my editor: I love your quip little comments and the way you polish my words. Thank you for all of the work you do for my stories.

My proofreader Karina: The way you catch small errors I've overlooked a hundred times blows my mind. Thank you for taking the time to read my stories.

My ARC readers: you are the very first set of eyes on my book baby once I let it out into the 'wild'. Your emails and PMs are always welcomed. Thank you for your support.